Cookies, Corpses and the

Deadly Haunt

A Bohemian Lake Cozy Mystery

Haunted House Flippers

In memory of Grump, who loved to work with his hands.

Haunted House Flippers Inc.
Cookies, Corpses & the Deadly Haunt
Candy Canes, Corpses & the Gothic Haunt
Crumb Cake, Corpses & the Run-of-the-Mill
Crème Eggs, Corpses & the Farmhouse Fixer
Black Cats, Corpses & the Pumpkin Pantry
New Prequel:
Christmas, Corpses & the Gingerbread Flip Flop

Rachael Stapleton

~

Hello and welcome to the wacky world of Bohemian Lake which just so happens to be my home away from home. I hope that you find it just as wonderful. And if you love HGTV and solving mysteries as much as I do then I'm sure you will. I started writing this book—the first in the House Flipper series on a whim several years ago. Just like my main character, Juniper, I'd come to a new town to live in a spooky old Victorian. That's right, the house in this story is based on my own second empire. But I'll save that story for the end.

Since this is the first book in a growing series with more to come, please make sure you sign up for my newsletter to get notifications on when the next book is ready. You can sign up for my newsletter here and as a bonus, receive a free copy of the Haunted House Flipper prequel: Christmas, Corpses and the Gingerbread Flip Flop!

Alright, let's wander some spooky old houses and solves mysteries together.

With much gratitude,

Rachael

ABOUT THIS BOOK

Cookies, Corpses and the Deadly Haunt is the first book in a haunting new paranormal cozy mystery series about house flippers living in the spirited world of Bohemian Lake.

Jack & Juniper agree to lend and help prep their latest purchase, an old Victorian mansion to act as the eerie setting for the town's Halloween bash. They're expecting to find missing floorboards, and pesky bats, not the ghostly specter of the murdered   Doctors   Wife.

But when the head of the council is found stuffed in a trunk in the attic, it appears history is repeating.

As Junie and the team, carry on with party preparations, they unravel a century of family secrets, whispers of lunacy, and the number one suspect goes on the run. Still, the victim's family insists that the ball must go on, even with a killer on the loose. With Halloween fast approaching, Junie sees the woman in white and wonders if keeping the killer out was ever really a possibility.

Now she's desperate to unmask the killer before the Annual Halloween Bash turns into even more of a deadly haunt...

ONE

Juniper Palmer cradled her lukewarm latte, looking past the dirty windowpanes and the swirling dust motes to the subtle scuffs and scratches of the run-down Victorian mansion she was about to tour. She'd yet to meet a historic home she didn't love, but there was something exceptional about this one.

And it wasn't just the rumored ghost.

No. It'd been love-at-first-sight four years ago when she'd happened upon it. From the moment she'd laid eyes on the still-intact Gothic Revival façade she'd felt something best described as a paranormal pull.

She ran her hand over a dent in the wall, thinking of the original owner. A disgraced physician, most famous for having murdered his blushing bride on all Hallows' Eve—a well-known tale in the small town that Juniper hoped would lighten the price tag.

The marks, themselves, were nothing out of the ordinary. All century homes acquired them. But in her mind, these were extraordinary. They were the signature and the soul of the very people who'd lived here, the murderous doctor and his ill-fated bride. *Were the rumors true? Was there a mystery here?*

Skeletal fingers tickled her spine with excitement.

Every blemish held a story, and Juniper was always up for a good story—especially if it was to be a ghost tale.

"It was a grand home once upon a time," Jared Mitchell, the fiftyish, plump, rather pallid realtor leading Juniper through the foyer said. Their usual realtor—her partner's father—was out of town and had arranged for the selling agent to show it.

"What happened to it?"

"It just needs a little TLC, but that's an easy task for renovating masters like yourself and your husband."

"Uh-huh," Juniper grunted. Jack Young was not her husband. He was her business partner and ex-boyfriend, but she wasn't in the mood to open that can of worms. Instead she put the focus back on the house. "TLC costs money, Mr. Mitchell, and this one requires a lot, not just a little, as you suggest," she said, feigning indifference.

The truth was she was already sold.

Juniper loved the widow's walk, the patterned shingle roof, and the location. This was a town of good people. Most of the residents of Bohemian Lake had here all of their lives, including her partner, Jack Young and her best-friend, Pike Hart. The cozy little town in upstate New York where entire generations of families were wed and buried in the stone church down the road would be an easy sell once they were ready to flip.

But that wasn't the only reason Juniper was interested.

The Doctor's House was begging for someone to put a little love back into it. And if the past few home renovations were any indication, she, or rather they, were the ones to do it. Still, she needed to play it cool if she wanted a better price. Spirited Construction had slowly started to turn a profit by restoring ghostly looking homes to their former glory and then flipping them. This one was pricey, but if they could make it work, then it would be their sixth.

Her best friend nudged her with her elbow and pointed. "Junie, just take a look at those moldings."

Juniper nodded. In the world of trim, crown was king. Lording high over casings, chair rails, and baseboards, and she'd already admired these ones with their soft edges and refined imperfections that characterized hand-carved work.

"It would make the most charming inn."

Pike was doing her best to sell Juniper on the place. "Charming, yet eerie," Juniper agreed.

Pike wrapped her hand around Juniper's arm and steered her into the dining room. Juniper's favorite thing about Victorian-era parlors and chambers were the paneled walnut pocket doors that discreetly separated them. Not that she'd admit that little fact to Jared. She paced across the room to one of the original leaded windows, then turned and stared up at the engraved plaster medallion and crystal chandelier. A common feature in the late 1800s—Jack would be so happy to see they remained.

"How many windows have been replaced?"

"Almost all of them. Aside from the two here in the front of the house and four in the kitchen, every other floor has been completely upgraded."

Juniper moved into the kitchen and quickly jotted down a basic layout. She was already reimaging a new one.

"And the wiring? There's no chance of knob and tube, is there?"

If there was one thing Juniper knew it was that modern home buyers did not go for knob and tube. They preferred their flickering lights be caused by sordid spirits than bad wiring. Those systems lacked the capacity for today's levels of power use and were prone to heat damage and fire. Not to mention insurance companies didn't charge premiums for ghosts, at least, not yet.

"None at all. It's all been removed."

"Good."

They kept walking. One room always led into the next in these old homes.

"Now, take a look at that carved limestone fireplace with the cupids." The realtor shook his balding head. "A real selling feature, don't you think? Most expensive property in town," Jared boasted. "Well worth it, for the right buyer. It's a massive home, with ten bedrooms. Ten. And this location is priceless, of course. Have you checked out the gardens on the hill? Not enough money in the world for something like that—what's not to love?"

"Yet you haven't been able to sell it," Juniper shot back. "I noticed graves back there. I'm not sure I'd like to flip a property with a cemetery attached. And well, it's just going to be so much work."

She was bluffing, of course. In comparison to their other jobs, this one would be a piece of cake as long as the ghost stayed in check. All it really needed was a new roof and kitchen. The bathrooms could use an update and the attic could be finished, but aside from that it was just wallpaper and paint. They didn't even need to replace the fixtures; those antiques were all in perfect working condition. It was what she and Jack called a spit polish, but she wasn't going to admit that.

The realtor's face grew a shade of red that matched the lips on Pike's rock-and-roll t-shirt. "That's where you come in. You're a general contractor, a partner of Spirited Construction. You and Jack specialize in renovating historic homes. Why not this one?"

"I don't know." Juniper walked away and examined the grand hallway and staircase. "I mean it's going to be a big project. The roof needs to be completely redone, and that's not cheap or easy on a mansard roof, especially considering the decorative style it would require and that kitchen looks pretty outdated."

Jared and Pike followed her out of the dining room and into the hall, and they walked toward the staircase.

"You have experience with that sort of thing, don't you?" He glanced desperately at Pike. "That's what I was told." Jared hedged. "You've flipped a few of these second empire houses before and made quite a profit from what I understand."

"And why hasn't it sold yet?" Juniper asked, feigning innocence as she wandered up the stairs. She knew why. But it was better to make the realtor admit it. She looked back at him.

"I'm not sure." His nose twitched, and he shuffled through the papers in his hands.

Pike smirked at her friend. She knew what Juniper was up to. For the past several decades, the Doctor's House had earned a reputation.

Juniper paused on the landing. "Jared… is there something people don't like about it—perhaps something that sends them running?"

"Well… some people consider it spooky." The tic in his nose sped up.

"You don't say." Juniper ran her hand along the bannister, removing a layer of dust to see the smooth wood beneath. "Black cats are spooky and people still love them. Is there something in particular people have a problem with?" Juniper asked.

"I can't say exactly."

Another long pause and then finally Juniper turned around to face him and said, "Well, we'd better go then. It was nice meeting you."

He stared wide-eyed back at Juniper, who'd moved to descend the stairs passed him. "Wait." His voice changed and she stopped to listen. "The ghosts, or whatever it is, appear to be running off prospective buyers. Every time there are clients touring the house, something... happens."

"What makes you think I want a haunted house?"

Jared shook his head. "Pike says you're fearless... and the best at what you do."

Just then Juniper heard a squeaking floorboard overhead and looked toward the ceiling above. It was coming from the third floor—the attic.

"Is someone else here?" she asked and climbed the rest of the way, coming to the second floor where a stained-glass window lit the area. The landing which was really a wide hallway had several doors that obviously led into other rooms, presumably bedrooms.

"That's what I'm talking about," Jared groused. He was breathing heavily now, having hurried after her.

Juniper listened carefully. She could hear music—a waltz.

"At least it's not death metal," she said with a chuckle.

Jared gave her a sour look.

"It starts and stops randomly throughout the day."

"And there's no other possible explanation? Who has access to the house?"

"Just my client and his wife Lucinda. She occasionally comes here. She's an Atherton. It's her family home. She inherited it, but there would be no reason for her to scare away potential buyers."

"True. Sabotage then? Do they have teenagers? Perhaps they like to play tricks."

"No kids. I don't really believe in this ghost stuff but most buyers are now refusing to even look at the place, so last month the owners called in help."

"Nana Vianu?" Pike questioned.

"Who's Nana Vianu?" Juniper asked.

"Oh sorry, Junie, I forget sometimes that you didn't grow up here. Nana Vianu owns the manor estate on Bohemian lake. Her granddaughter Mallory and her adopted daughter Danior run themed retreats and host murder mystery parties. It's basically an eccentric resort."

"So, why would the owners of this house have called in Nana to help with ghosts?"

"Oh right. Well, they're gifted. They descend from… err… well, they are a powerful group of women…"

"They're gypsies," Jared cut in.

"They're Roma, and that term is offensive!" Pike corrected.

"Roma, fine, whatever. They can see the future and talk to spirits and all that other voodoo."

"It's not voodoo," Pike corrected.

"Well, it's beside the point because they didn't call Nana or Mallory Vianu. They called the other medium. The younger girl from across town—the one who does the ghost tours and claims to commune with the dead."

"Who's that?" Juniper asked, thinking it odd that a small town required multiple mediums. Not that she doubted it. Juniper had already met one of Bohemian Lake's spirits.

"Her name escapes me at the moment. Marble or Emerald. You know her, Pike! She's friends with Axl and Kaitlyn Patone."

"Pearl?" Pike suggested.

"That's it!" the realtor said with a snap of his fingers. "Pearl Lourdes. Her family is new to town. They just moved here about five years ago."

"And that's new?" Juniper asked, entering one of the bedrooms and crossing to an old built in. The books on the shelves had all been left behind, caked with spider webs and the grime of neglect.

"It is for Bohemian Lake," Pike answered as she grabbed hold of thick velvet rose colored drapes and yanked. She coughed and spluttered for a moment before turning to face Jared. "You know, you should really get someone in here to dust. That would help sell the place."

Jared nodded. "Yes, unfortunately, the last three cleaners were scared away."

Juniper lifted her hand to hide her smile and turned her attention back to the bookshelf. Now that there was more light, a quick perusal revealed a history book on the Hudson Valley region as well as one more specifically dedicated to the town of Bohemian Lake. She'd have to check those out later. There was also a ton of old mystery novels and one of her favorites, Mary Shelley's Frankenstein.

"Nice selection," she said and turned back to face the realtor and Pike. "So, what did Pearl make of the Doctor's House?"

Again, with the tic. Jared pinched and held the bridge of his nose for a moment. "Pearl says the ghosts of the family that used to live here are angry that it's been neglected. She says the only way to appease them is to sell the house to someone who will love and restore it."

"I see," Juniper said, continuing her exploration of the second floor. Either Jared was making that up to appeal to her, or she was right and this house needed her. Either way, it was a good fit.

Once or twice she thought she heard—or felt—wisps of conversations just out of reach of hearing, although she searched her peripheral vision and no ghosts appeared. Perhaps the ghosts were never trying to scare anyone off and only living their life without realizing the passage of time had forsaken them.

To the left of the hall was another set of stairs. Juniper stepped back, just missing Pike's toes. She was freezing cold.

"What is it?" Pike asked. "You feel that draft?"

Juniper nodded. "It must be coming from the attic?" she said, heading up. This third floor staircase was much steeper and narrower than the main one.

There were three doors at the top. One on each side of the staircase that were open and one door directly in front that was closed.

Juniper stepped into the room through the left doorway, while Pike stepped into the right, allowing Jared to catch up and take the lead. He was wheezing pretty good.

"Why is this staircase so scary and what happens if you aren't a toothpick?" Pike questioned.

Juniper laughed. "Only the servants would have bunked up here, Pike. And I don't think the elite were overly concerned about them. If they didn't fit, then they weren't hired, that would be my guess."

"Exactly. The rooms you're standing in were the former servants' quarters, and this—," Jared said, reaching for the door handle. He rattled the knob. "Dammit! Who locked it?"

"Maybe the ghosts," Juniper teased.

He glared at her as though she had been egging on the spirits to get a better price—perhaps she had.

"It's alright. I've seen enough," Juniper stated.

"So, how soon can we sign the paperwork?" Jared asked as they descended the stairs.

Juniper stayed silent all the way down to the main floor, making the man sweat. Jared was a little much, and she enjoyed toying with him.

She watched him jangle his car keys—BMW, of course.

Number one rule for negotiating? Imply that you're too busy. She sucked air in between her teeth and shook her head slowly.

"I'm gonna be honest, Jared. The Doctor's House has been neglected. To restore it would take a fair chunk of change, and to do it right would take time. Time is not the house flipper's friend. Now we are always interested in a challenge but Spirited Construction is pretty busy. I'll let you know once I've spoken to Jack, my partner, but the truth is we weren't looking to take on another property at the moment. We're finishing up a Georgian Revival in Lakeside and we've still got a crew on a retreat in—"

"What if I can talk my clients into dropping the price?"

Juniper took a moment, looked around, then nodded slowly. The actual truth was they were finished with all of their projects and completely ready to make the next purchase, but it never hurt to play hardball. "All right. I think I can help you out but I need to call my—"

Juniper cut herself off as she saw something out of the corner of her eye.

It was a dark-haired woman in a light lace dress creeping up the mansion's front steps. A gush of wind sent fallen leaves dancing down the steps around her. She was pale as a ghost.

Could this be the ghost of the manor, bound to toil in the Doctor's House mansion throughout eternity?

TWO

J uniper's eyes bulged at the ghostly figure who was now stepping through the mansion's front door.

"Kaitlyn!" Jared called out. "Let me introduce you. This is Juniper Palmer. Juniper is interested in the mansion—we were just about to settle on a price. Weren't we Juniper?" This was obviously a rhetorical question because the man didn't even pause to let Juniper answer. "Juniper, Kaitlyn's from one of Bohemian Lake's most prominent families and she is heavily involved in the community. As a matter of fact, her father is the mayor and her mother chairs several of our boards."

Not a phantom specter, then. Juniper relaxed, taking inventory of the woman before her. Pale and tall, she wore thick black glasses, and hunched—almost as if she were trying to dim her own good looks. Why else would a woman so young dress so matronly?

Kaitlyn shook Juniper's hand, and they exchanged pleasantries; then Juniper gave her a business card.

"You're a handy woman," Kaitlyn said after studying it.

"I guess that's one way to put it. I specialize in restoring historic homes and re-selling them."

"Are you planning to fix up the Doctor's house, then?"

"If we can come to an agreement, then yes."

Kaitlyn's cell phone beeped. "That's great news for the town. I hope you'll consider letting us use it for the Haunted Ball. That's our annual Halloween Fundraiser and we're looking for an extra special venue this year."

"Were you looking for something here today, Kaitlyn?" Jared asked.

Kaitlyn cast a wary glance at Jared. "No, I thought I saw my mother head in this direction but I guess she was just cutting across the lawn to get to Fern's. Anyway, I'm sorry to rush off, but I'm late for an appointment. I hope to see you again."

"Definitely. If Spirited Construction purchases the house, then I'll be spending plenty of time here," Juniper said.

"Great." Kaitlyn's phone beeped again, and she checked the screen. "I'm sorry. I really have to run. I have a meeting at the Historical Society. Nice to meet you, Juniper. Please consider what I said about the fundraiser. The Doctor's Mansion would be the perfect venue."

Another cautious glance in the direction of the stairs, then she left through the front entrance, a beautiful wood door with stained glass panels.

THREE

Pike, the newly appointed lead of the town's Halloween fundraising project, flexed her fingers around the hilt of the pickaxe before slamming the prop down against the attic's floorboards.

Juniper set aside her tablet where she'd been perusing stainless steel appliances and countertop samples for the new kitchen install, and winced. "You're going to break something and I don't want to pay for it."

"If only it were Kaitlyn's face," she said, swinging the Halloween prop once again.

Thankfully the clickity-clack of Kaitlyn's heels on the stairs below grew more and more distant.

"I can't believe that snooty witch had the nerve to comment on my leadership." Pike paced the attic floor.

"You mean, 'lack thereof', don't you?" Juniper teased, quoting Kaitlyn from only moments ago.

Pike practically growled. "I can't believe her!"

"I can't believe a lot of things that have happened in the last two weeks. Like the bill from the roofing company or this," Juniper said, bending over to scoop up the present that Kaitlyn's mangy mutt had left behind. "Who lets their dog go to the bathroom in someone's house?"

"Right?! That poor little terrier deserves a better role model than her."

Juniper was thinking obedience class or some sort of training but shrugged and allowed Pike to continue her rant.

"Next time, I swear I'm going to use this on her." Pike shook the plastic axe. Her long hair, swept up into a topknot and perched loosely at the crown of her head, went lopsided.

Juniper ran her fingers through her own platinum bob, smoothing a piece of hair at the front and walked to the window. Getting Pike's feathers riled took a special kind of person, which was probably why the town council had asked Pike to take over. Kaitlyn had managed to tick off almost every volunteer during her two-week reign of terror. Juniper leaned her forehead against the glass and peered down through the half-bare leaves of the oak tree in the front yard. She was just in time to see Kaitlyn and her terrorizing little terrier get into the passenger side of a shiny red Camaro.

Or at least that's what it looked like through the cluster of metallic, bristly bodied blowflies as they buzzed and crawled all over the attic's grimy window.

"The way they hover like that…" she pointed to the creepy blowflies with their huge orange eyes just as one of the darted into her face. She backed up, nearly tripping over an antique blue trunk.

"It's creepy isn't it? Like something out of Amityville or American Horror Story," Pike said, finally calming and returning to her happy self. She threw the axe aside and picked up a box of scary clown parts. The jointed figure slumped inward as she set it on a table, glass eyes wide open. "Anyway, I need to forget about Kaitlyn and focus on the amazing event we're going to throw. It's been forever since we celebrated Halloween properly in this town."

"How come?"

"Good question. I don't really know. I was a teenager. All the events were held by this one family but then their daughter had an accident and they just stopped."

"Did she die?"

"Not sure. I never see them around anymore, so maybe. They used to go all out with a scary pumpkin patch and a haunted barn. It was the best but this is gonna be just as good. And it's all thanks to you."

"Oh, it's no big deal, Pike," Juniper lied.

Of course, it was a bit of a big deal. She and Jack had been forced to re-jig some of their plans after agreeing but it had all worked out. They'd decided to focus on the exterior in the first couple of weeks. Jack had come first, overseeing the roofing company, reinforcing the porches and dealing with some minor structural issues. After that, he and the crew had demolished the old kitchen.

On most flips, they also replaced or at least updated the baths but given that all the mechanicals were working well, they'd decided to hold off until after the Halloween event.

"Do you know how many times I rode by as a kid and wished I could see inside? It is going to make for one heck of a Halloween bash."

The town's council, particularly Helen, Kaitlyn's mother, had pounced as soon as Spirited Construction made the purchase. They'd wisely sent Pike to talk Juniper into lending it for the Halloween Ball. Apparently, attendance had been low the last nine years, ever since they moved in from the Sleepy Hollow Estate outside of town. They thought with it being the one-hundred-year anniversary of the Doctor's house murder, they could drum up ticket sales using morbid curiosity. Juniper suspected the publicity would be good for Spirited Construction—not to mention she was secretly macabre obsessed, so what could be better than spending Halloween in a house rumored to be haunted.

Pike leaned against one of the open beams. "This attic is just so naturally creepy. Doing a haunted house up here in addition to the ball downstairs was good thinking. The teenagers are going to love it." Pike picked up the scissors. "So how do I make this ghost again?"

"Start wrapping the tape around the mannequin and we'll stick an LED light in there when you're done." Juniper took a sip of the spiced pumpkin latte Pike had brought her from her coffee shop, Cookies & Corsets.

"How's business, anyway?" Juniper asked over the squeak of the tape. "I can't wait to check it out. I think it's so neat that you share the space with a vintage dress shop."

"It's only been six months, but so far it's great." Her blue-green eyes clouded over. "Of course, the building is possibly being sold."

"What? Why?"

"The owners, Lulu and Peter are having problems."

"Lulu owns the dress shop, right?"

"Mm-hmm, they also own the building. I think they're heading for separation. It's been a war zone all week." Pike shook her head. "Poor Lulu. She tries to hide it, but she's heartbroken. She thinks Peter is having an affair and now he's in talks to sell the building. To the mayor of all people! Like Frank needs to get his grubby little hands on anything else in this town." Pike shook her head. "I don't know what I'll do if that happens. Lulu doesn't want to sell. It's taken her a long time to get her vintage clothing business off the ground, but Peter doesn't seem to care."

"You can't take on other people's problems, Pike. Anyway, won't the Mayor let you stay? Share the space perhaps, the way Lulu does."

Her face twisted in disgust. "Hell to the no! Even if he did, I wouldn't. You see, apparently, Mayor Patone has plans to open up a pizza parlor for his kids to run. It's bad enough I have to put up with that uptight little snot bag, Kaitlyn, in regard to this project… soon she'll be stealing my shop."

Juniper frowned. Pike had worked non-stop since college saving every last penny to open that bakery. It would be a shame if it all slipped away now.

"It's too far-fetched to even consider, but I wish I could buy the building. Sadly, I can barely afford to rent it after buying all new appliances."

Juniper snorted. "I hear you. It's nice to have a business partner, but I wish I could have afforded this place on my own."

Pike's eyes lit up. "Why? So, you could open up the Charming Little Inn? It is so close to the wineries—you could advertise to the upper crust winos."

Juniper smiled. This was a game they often indulged in—who could dream bigger. "Yes, and you could move your coffee shop in."

"Wouldn't that be nice!"

"Believe me, I've thought it over, but I've got my hands full with this construction business. Maybe after a couple more flips, we'll have broken into the high-end historic-home-renovation business. Then Jack can buy me out and we can finally go our separate ways."

"Right. Like you and Jack actually want to separate. I've never seen more amicable exes."

"What choice do we have? We own this company together and neither one of us can afford to buy the other out."

"Is that why you both spend so much time together?"

"We can't afford all that much additional help."

"Did someone say help?"

The mayor's son climbed the stairs into the attic. Axl was a ruggedly handsome twenty-something with a rich frat boy vibe. He was always hitting on Pike and getting rejected. "Where should I put the stiff?" He joked, referring to the life-size doll he clutched in his arms.

"Right over there with the trunk and the chainsaw is fine," Juniper instructed. We're going to outline it in chalk and put up yellow caution tape.

"Where did that come from? It looks familiar," Axl commented.

Juniper looked at the beat-up blue trunk that she'd almost fell over earlier. "I don't know. It was here when we took possession. It was originally up in the rafters, but someone must have brought it down last night or this morning."

"Do you think it's *the trunk*?" Axl asked.

"Huh?" Juniper questioned.

Pike, who had been sitting on it, suddenly stood up and moved away. "I hardly think a one hundred-year-old chest that once housed the dead body of the doctor's wife would still be here."

"Oh, that trunk," Juniper said, cluing in to the rumored murder that had taken place.

"Is it locked? Let's pop that bad boy open and have a look-see." Axl walked toward it.

"Later. We still have a lot to do." On top of helping with the decorations, Juniper still had her regular house flipping tasks to finish like stripping wallpaper, installing new tile and shopping for fixtures.

"Fine," Axl relented, setting the dummy on the trunk. "I'll go bring up the rest of the decorations."

From outside, Juniper heard the sounds of hammering. They'd accomplished so much in the last couple of weeks but there was still so much more to do. She walked to the window and wrenched it open. The crisp, clear October air hit her, tickling her neck. The smell brought back some of her favorite memories of times when she would visit Jack here in his hometown, spending time alone in the woods, or strolling through his parent's vineyard. She closed her eyes to let the sweet, sharp smell of the fallen leaves block out all other sensations and when she opened them, she saw that Jack was busy replacing the rotting floorboards on the porch. Her heart beat even faster. It had been four years since they'd split and the feelings still hadn't eased. They'd met through Pike at first, which had led to Jack working the summers for Juniper's dad's construction company. At twenty-two, fresh out of school, they'd opened Spirited Construction with Juniper's father's help and had great success. In two years, they'd flipped two houses and bought a third and then Jack had proposed marriage. Pressured by his friends and family, he'd done it here in his hometown on Christmas Eve. Juniper was still modeling part-time and was due to leave on assignment for a month and in a moment of panic, she'd rejected him. They broke up and when she returned, he was already dating one of his old school chums, Sally.

Juniper shook her head in disbelief. So much water under the bridge, but they'd pushed past it and their relationship and business were better than ever, except for the fact that he was now engaged to Sally, the devil's hand-maiden.

"Hey," Pike interrupted. She was kneeling on a built-in window seat, looking out the bay window over the back. "I think I saw someone go into the garden."

Juniper shut the front window and walked over to where Pike was kneeling. "Yeah, you probably did. We have a landscaper helping out today."

"I can't see a landscaper dressing like this."

Axl, who'd just returned with another cardboard box joined Pike and Juniper at the back window, just in time to see a woman in an antique white dress disappear behind a tall, gnarly, old oak tree. It was broad daylight. A chill wrapped itself around the top of Juniper's spine and slid down like a fireman's pole.

Outside, the hammering stopped. It was replaced by the sound of a creepy violin coming from downstairs. Juniper looked hard, but she could no longer see the woman in white.

They all froze and looked at one another.

Axl spoke first. "Was that the Doctor's wife?"

Pike backhanded him in the belly. "Shhh! Don't say things like that in here. Are you trying to get us killed?" Her eyes were darting back and forth like she was searching the ghost out. Footsteps sounded from the floor below. And though the music had stopped, the quiet was almost worse.

"You don't have to be scared," Axl said. "The neighbors have reported seeing a ghost here for a long time."

"Easy for you to say," Juniper shot back. "You don't sleep here."

"Honestly, she never hurts anyone."

The overhead light decided at that moment to flicker out.

"Bad sign," Pike said.

"No, let's get back to reality. It's just old wiring," Juniper responded.

The dummy which Axl had left propped in a sitting position on top of the trunk fell over with a loud bang.

They all jumped.

"Break time!" Pike shouted. "Let's hit up my place."

Juniper couldn't agree more. As they hurried down the stairs, the panic lifted and Juniper started to feel better.

It was crazy to think how easy it was to get sucked in to the hysteria of old ghost stories.

Juniper looked around as they came to the front door. "Where'd Axl go?" They turned and heard the back door close. "I guess he's not coming with us."

Pike shrugged. "He probably has a hot lunch date. I bet he gets more action in a week then you've seen in two years."

"Oh, good. So, it's nose into Juniper's sad love life day, huh? How about we talk about that woman in the garden—did that really just happen?"

"I don't know. She was so far away. I guess maybe it could have been one of the neighbors taking a stroll. Maybe Kaitlyn's trying to scare us off."

"Yeah, really."

"It was a pretty dress though, which is what you need to wear sometimes."

"Oh yeah, you think Jack would appreciate his business partner coming to a jobsite in a frilly old gown. I'm not sure it would be very conducive to climbing ladders."

"Yeah, yeah. All I'm saying is put on a dress once in a while and remind Jack of what he's missing."

Juniper looked over at Pike, whose outfit matched her own—white top, torn jeans with the ankles cuffed and brown beat-up motorcycle boots.

"Well maybe people in glass houses shouldn't throw stones. You were awful grouchy to Miss Patone this morning. Wanna talk about all that repressed sexual energy?"

Pike had her arms crossed, and a stubborn frown crinkled her forehead. "Don't try to turn the tables on me. You told me to wear this. I wear frilly tops and dresses every other day. We're talking about you right now—the yummy things that tempt you every day."

"Are you talking about pizza? 'Cause that's tempting. When is that parlor opening up again?"

Pike fake punched Juniper on the arm as they started down the front walkway. "You'll just have to settle for sandwiches and pumpkin pie cookies."

"You still make those? They were my favorite."

"Of course, and they're much better now."

Juniper glanced over her shoulder as she shrugged on her thick cardigan, taking in the imposing red brick mansion. Only half listening to Pike, as they crossed the road. This house checked all the boxes to make it spooky: eyebrow dormers set into a mansard roof, an iron widow's walk, and a ghost, and yet Juniper still couldn't help but find it beautiful especially with the new scalloped roof. Those bluish violet shingles had been pricey but worth it. *My house*, Juniper thought with a bit of pride. Well, half mine, she amended. There was always Jack to consider. Still, Juniper wished they didn't have to sell it; there was something different about this place, or was it just that it was Jack's hometown?

She sighed and moved on.

***

Pike's shop, Cookies & Corsets was covered in cornstalks and Jack-o'-lanterns on the outside and jammed with old fashioned booths, baked goods and clothing racks on the inside. The place smelled like heaven, a favorable combination of fresh laundry, coffee and vanilla bean.

It was two stores operating out of one storefront, just like the name. The lighting was soft and flattering and the space was separated by a decorative wall of beads that was pulled back so shoppers could grab a coffee and peruse. Where Pike's shelves were crowded with fancy plates and coffee cups, Lulu's side held shoes and purses.

"I see Prince Charming is still pining for you," Pike whispered into Juniper's ear.

Juniper's eyes focused on Jack as he paid for his lunch at the counter, a thatch of dark hair flopped over one eye. Her mouth quirked up, "Prince Charming, huh?" Juniper wondered how in the world a long-ago boyfriend who'd dumped her for Sally-big-boobs qualified as that.

"Hey, I think the situation is weird myself, but you're the one who's still got a thing for him." With an amused glint in her eyes, Pike leaned forward. "Afterall, you had no problem picking up on who I was referring to."

"I had a fifty-fifty chance. He is one out of only two men in the store, and the other man is thirty years my senior."

"Don't knock Harold. You should see that man dance. His comb-over is legendary—it doesn't even move."

"Most impressive and now you've gone and sold me on him. Eat your heart out, Jack Young, I am trading you in."

"Oh, sorry. I may have oversold Harold. Also, his wife Joanne may have something to say about it. Then again, they were big on Woodstock."

Juniper laughed at Pike's jokes and pretended it was all just light-hearted fun but the truth was, Pike was right. Jack had stolen her heart once upon a time, and though they'd moved beyond the awkward phase, she still carried a torch.

"This is exciting! So exciting, isn't it?"

Juniper turned to see who was interrupting them. It was the Mayor's wife, Helen, looking Stepford chic—as Pike called it—in a white butterfly tea dress that had surely come from an Audrey Hepburn yard sale.

Juniper had heard one of the locals call her a chihuahua with a penchant for sugar and gossip, and now she couldn't get the image out of her head. It was so fitting. Helen did remind her of just that, a tiny dog that stood at the fence and incessantly barked.

Helen elbowed her way forward and lifted the lid on the glass case, stealing one of Pike's specialty pumpkin cookies. Pike's employee, a young girl with a dark Betty Page bob and glasses rolled her eyes at Helen's back. With her perfectly coiffed hair, Helen wore her privilege like she wore her single strand of pearls. She smiled wide like an ex-sorority sister, the sort who took pleasure in torturing all the other girls.

Juniper couldn't help but think how very different Helen was from her daughter. They were both rude but where Kaitlyn was tall, dark and muscular; Helen was petite, fair and soft.

"Okay, I'll bite, Helen. What's so exciting?" Pike asked after Helen repeated herself for the fourth time.

"You girls… you saw the ghost! Honestly, Pike, don't be so thick," Helen chided.

Juniper furrowed her brows. How did Helen know they'd seen something? Pike and Jack had both implied she was a busybody, but this was next level. Either she was psychic, or she employed spies.

Pike turned away from Helen and instead addressed the smiling, tall and curvy woman across the room, "Lulu, you remember my friend, Junie?"

"Of course." Lulu motioned excitedly. Green gauze fluttered out behind her as she crossed the shop floor to give Juniper a lavender-and-vanilla-scented hug. "It's all anyone can talk about. What a pleasure! My, my, aren't you still just as pretty?" she gushed.

"Thank you," Juniper said, a bit startled, but flattered by her warm welcome. "It's nice to see you again."

Juniper had briefly met Lulu back in the day when she and Jack had dated. Lulu had been a beautiful woman then, and she still was, however Pike was right about her looking stressed. Her thin face was puffy and her once bright green eyes were dull and red, not to mention the slightly glazed-over look to them.

"How goes the renovation?" Helen interrupted. "Is our favorite haunted mansion going to be ready on time?"

"Of course," Jack said with a boyish grin as he winked. "Junie and I have never missed a deadline. Have we Junie?"

Juniper smiled but shook her head at him like he was a naughty child. The man had no sense of jinxes and self-preservation. Jack took this as his cue to leave and glided out quietly behind another customer. Juniper scowled in his direction then smiled at Helen—public relations was apparently Juniper's job.

"I hope so! I just got into town today, but Jack and our crew have been working on it for weeks. And Pike, and even your Kaitlyn have been in there helping to decorate. Of course, as much as we've got done, there is still a lot to do."

Helen leaned forward in her chair, clasping her hands primly together. "And the… uh… ghost… what was she doing?"

"Well, we don't know that it was a ghost for sure. It could have been a woman. A neighbor just walking in the garden. We only saw her for half a second," Juniper replied, pulling the lapels of her sweater a little closer around her.

"Before she disappeared… that's just what I heard. This is so exciting!" Helen repeated with a happy sigh, clapping her hands together as though Christmas was coming early. "I wonder what she wants."

"What who wants?" Harold asked.

"The ghost of Victoria."

"Oh, that's just hooey." Harold barked.

Pike seemed to notice Lulu's discomfiture. "So, Lulu, we need costumes for the ball," she said, readying a tray of cookies on the counter.

Helen gave Harold a shove out of the way and crossed to Lulu. "I've just had a brilliant idea. Halloween is the anniversary of the murder. Don't you think our new owners would make the perfect Doctor and his wife?" Pike practically choked on a piece of her blueberry muffin but Helen didn't even pause. "Then again, you and Jack are not really a couple anymore, are you? I suppose Sally would object."

"Have you seen the ghost?" Juniper asked Helen, walking over to pat Pike on the back. She'd done nothing to keep the sharpness from her voice and wondered if Miss Sorority would notice.

"Not exactly. Kaitlyn has seen things on occasion, and the neighbor's daughter has been visited frequently, but I'm afraid I'm much too normal to see such things."

"Normal, my—," Pike mumbled the end.

"Pardon me, Pike? I'm afraid you need to learn to enunciate like a grownup."

"Glass. Sorry this glass is dirty. I need to clean it."

Juniper looked at Pike and smirked.

"Are you okay, Lulu?" Helen blurted.

Juniper looked back at Lulu whose olive toned face was white.

Lulu nodded silently, but side stepped as if she'd lost her balance.

"Are you sure?" Juniper asked with trepidation. "Maybe you should sit—" She approached the woman who then tumbled over with a slight thud, nearly taking down a large urn full of parasols and umbrellas.

"Lulu," Helen said, cutting in front of Juniper as she rushed over. She kneeled down next to her cousin and pressed her hand against Lulu's forehead. "Are you okay?"

Lulu squeezed her eyes shut and Helen responded by prying one eyelid open with her thumb.

Lulu twisted her head around and batted her hand away. "Get your damn fingers out of my face, Helen. Seriously, what are you doing?"

"I don't know, checking to see if you passed out."

"I'm fine. I'm sitting up for goodness' sake. I fell on my butt that's no cause for hysterics." She muttered, pushing Helen away. She turned to Pike, who'd also come over. "Help me up, would you, doll?"

Pike bent down and helped Lulu to her feet.

"Have you eaten today?" Helen asked. She turned to Juniper. "Silly thing. She's always forgetting to eat."

"Of course, I've eaten. What am I, an idiot?" she said a bit too quickly. "Fine. Everything's fine."

Helen lifted one eyebrow. "Is it Peter?"

Lulu's eye's teared up. "No. I think I just ate some bad sushi last night or something. It's passed."

Pike patted her hand. "Why don't you go lay on the cot in the back and I'll man the store for you."

"I said I'm fine, everyone. Thank you but I don't need to be treated like some helpless crazy person."

Juniper and Pike exchanged a look. *Where had that come from?*

"She's fine. Just let her be," Helen said, as Lulu stomped off to the back.

Juniper turned back to Helen. "How did you know that we'd seen a ghost? It only just happened."

"Axl called to inform me, which reminds me, I'm late to take him his lunch."

"Take him his lunch? He's twenty years old."

"I know. Boys just need their mothers, don't they? I'll see you both at the party tonight, right?"

Shoot! Juniper had forgotten about Helen's birthday party. She knew there was a reason she wasn't planning to arrive in town until tomorrow.

"I'm not sure I can make it," Juniper called back. "There's so much to do over at the house still."

"Well, you can't very well work on things at night, now can you?"

Actually, she could and she did quite often, but she didn't bother pointing that out. A socialite like Helen who'd been born with a silver stick up her butt, would hardly understand.

"Anyway, Jack and Sally are coming to dance the night away. It's hardly fair that you should be left behind to slave away, now is it?"

"No, it's not," Juniper agreed, grudgingly.

"Besides, it will give you the opportunity to wear one of those pretty outfits you used to wear on the covers of the magazines. Get you out of that manly work ensemble. I mean, really, you must hate having to dress like that."

Pike snickered.

Juniper looked down. *What was everyone's problem today?* These were her favorite buttonfly jeans.

"Bring a date if you want, although I hear that new detective in town is single. He was chasing Penny Trubble from the newspaper but she turned him down. Her loss is your gain, I say! Anyway, tootaloo," Helen said, swirling out of the store like a tornado in full swing.

FOUR

Several hours later, Juniper locked up the mansion and headed down the front steps in a white jumpsuit, nude ankle boots and a fringed black leather jacket. She'd applied some makeup and added some beach waves to her wispy blonde hair in the hopes it would appease the town's resident fashion police. In other words, she hoped it would keep Helen's barbed comments in check.

Darkness had settled like a thick blanket over the town of Bohemian Lake. Fallen leaves danced in the wind around the pumpkins on the porch. She was just stepping onto the sidewalk when a small group of people approached the house. The two teenage girls in front had on coats advertising the town's haunted tour.

"Is it true what they say about this place?" a purple-haired girl wearing a leather coat and paisley scarf asked. The girl held her flashlight under her chin, casting a glow on her face and making the braces on her teeth gleam.

"That it's haunted? Yes," One of the leaders of the group said with a serious face. "The Ghost Hunters Association listed this house as one of the most haunted places in North America." The tour leader gestured toward Juniper's lovely old gothic Victorian.

With widened eyes, the group followed the direction of her pointing finger.

Juniper turned around and approached them. "Excuse me? Are you giving a ghost tour?"

"I am. This is your house now, right? You're Juniper Palmer." The girl extended her hand. "I'm Pearl. My friend told me about you."

Juniper nodded. "Do you mind if I listen in? I'd love to hear what you have to say."

"I'd be honored." The girl projected her voice so the people at the back could here. "Can I get your attention, everyone? This is the doctor's house, which is rumored to be haunted by the 19th-century family who built it. Apparitions, whispers, footsteps and cold spots have been reported throughout the house and property," Pearl said. "The spirit of a woman is often seen roaming the grounds. Her silhouette appears as a white misty form."

A woman clung trembling to her date's arm. Her eyes widened as Pearl continued her story. *What was someone like that doing on a ghost tour?* Juniper had a feeling if the ghostess of the manor appeared tonight, that shaky woman would be the first to pee her pants and run away. The man, on the other hand had his arms crossed and folded across his chest in a disbelieving manor.

"Isn't there a legend that says on Halloween the Doctor and his wife come alive?" asked one of the group participants.

Juniper's gaze shot back to Pearl.

"Yes, there is a rumor that the tormented ghost of the Doctor-turned-murderer and his bride appear on the anniversary date and the murder plays out, like it did on that fateful Halloween. But you should know Victoria and her husband weren't the only ones to die in this house."

"Well, that's convenient for business, isn't it?" the standoffish man scoffed.

Several people laughed then the group looked around at one another and fell back into silence.

"Victoria's brother-in-law tried to sell the place after the murder-suicide but no one would buy it." Pearl went on. "Then a huge fire hit the town, and they lost the saw mill.

The man couldn't take it anymore. He was found inside the foyer, swinging from the massive chandelier.

"He killed himself?" Juniper blurted.

"So, it would appear."

Great. Just… great, Juniper thought, doing a mental head slap. Another death. Why hadn't they asked for a detailed history before agreeing to purchase? Didn't realtors need to disclose this sort of information?

"Was it the ghost who killed him?" The purple-haired girl who'd spoken first earlier, whispered.

"Maybe." Pearl guided the group across the grass to the stone path that led back to the entrance.

The girl who worked alongside Pearl spoke up, "Okay, everyone if you could follow me. We're going to take a quick break inside the café where the owner has hot beverages and snacks prepared for us before she closes and after that we'll head to our final stop for the night, the graveyard."

Pearl turned to Juniper. "Nice meeting you. If you're ever interested in having us, we love taking the tour guests inside."

Juniper nodded. "I'll think about it."

***

As soon as the crowd dispersed, Juniper walked down the street. Bohemian Lake had one main drag—Main Street—with various avenues leading off of it like fish ribs off a spine. She looked around for a library but didn't immediately see one. It would be good to do a little research and find out more about that family. If there'd been more than one murder then it would surely come up with buyers when they went to flip it.

Oh well, she'd save that for another day. Her plate was full enough at the moment.

Helen and Frank Patone lived on one of the back streets in a mostly residential area where the bulk of the houses were small and boxy Craftsman Bungalows. Juniper loved the details on them. Low-pitched gable roof with deep, bracketed overhangs and exposed rafters. The porches were her favorite with their massive piers for support. They were so cute and inviting. Every now and then she'd see a Foursquare Craftsman mixed in. Which was basically the same just made for larger families. They were the bigger, plainer cousins of the Craftsman bungalow and became popular after the First World War.

It was quiet on the back street, except for the random ringing of church bells, and when a breeze picked up, it carried the smell of fresh-baked bread from Main Street. Juniper was just passing by the Boho Assisted Living Village when she heard voices coming from the bushes.

She swiveled her head to the right and spotted an older man in slippers on the other side of the bush. "What are you after? Smokes, tokes, sweets?" whispered one of the voices. "I've also got hooch, whip cream and girlie posters."

"I'll take the whipped cream and what the hell, give me one of your calendars too."

Juniper stepped forward, peering behind the bush. The woman who worked the desk at Bohemian Lake's newspaper was perched on a gardening stool, an inventory list in one hand and a pen in the other. Her hair was long, and most of her face was lost behind a pair of enormous square-framed sunglasses.

"Mrs. Banter? Is that you?"

The man grabbed his brown bag, shoved a bill into her hand and scuttled away as quick as a man with a cane wearing slippers could.

"Juniper, dear. How the heck are you?"

"I'm good. Just heading to the Patones' estate for that party."

Mrs. Banter rolled her eyes. "You poor girl. I have just the thing for that." She reached into her bag of contraband and pulled out a bottle of liquid Tylenol. "Take this and slug it back before you pass through the gate. Trust me, it'll help."

"Liquid Tylenol. Why would I need that, Mrs. Banter?"

"Oh please, call me Eve, dear. Mrs. Banter was my last husband's mother."

Juniper chuckled. She had recently learned that Mrs. Banter had been married three times, and she was looking for her fourth. She was a real spitfire. Juniper's overriding hope in life was to have as much spirit as her in her golden years.

"Okay, Eve. Why would I need children's Tylenol? I don't even have a headache yet."

"Oh, but you will. Just swig it. Trust me. It's on the house."

Juniper uncapped the bottle and took a swig and then coughed. "Good lord that was not Tylenol." Juniper coughed again. "Is that whiskey or wine? I'm so confused."

"Brandy, actually. I make my own."

Juniper wiped at her eyes with the sleeve of her leather jacket. "That is potent stuff. Are you trafficking contraband into the old age home?"

"Shh!" she hissed. "You're gonna give me away to the man?"

"What man? There's a man after you?"

"Please girl, what man or woman in this place isn't after me but that's not what I mean. I'm hiding out. That ball busting nurse, Rebel Jones is after me."

"Rebel Jones? I don't think I've met her."

"Oh no, there's one of them now. Got to go," she said with a growl. Then she grabbed her big bag and whipped past Juniper, leaving a faint smell of lemon verbena and pressed face powder. Juniper shook off the cloying heavy smell as if it were water and continued walking until she reached the Patone's backyard gate.

Of course, she wasn't surprised at all to stumble upon the Patones' house which was completely different from the others. Set in the middle of this cute street, their mansion stuck out like a sore thumb. It was, in her opinion, as tacky as them. It even had a guesthouse which was just a smidge smaller than the main house. That was where she'd heard Kaitlyn lived.

White and silver balloons covered every available surface while party lights and a sparkling disco ball hung from the pergola. To Juniper's eye, it looked more like a wedding reception than a birthday party.

Juniper sighed. Good thing she'd gone with the white jumpsuit. Hopefully she could blend in. This was the last place she wanted to be. Once upon a time, she would have looked forward to a party with Pike and Jack and all of their friends. Of course, that was before Big Boobs, the bane of her existence, stole Jack away. Now, she'd just get her nose rubbed in it.

She had hoped when she agreed to flip the Doctors house that she could avoid being pulled back into Jack's notorious social circle, but she should have known better.

Juniper carefully looked around for Pike as more and more people filtered in. A nice secluded table is just what she needed.

"Juniper, is that you?"

Juniper quietly swore to herself. She immediately recognized the voice.

"Juniper! Didn't you hear me?" Sally asked. "I called your name back there."

Juniper's normally serene face hardened, as she pivoted to face the other woman. "Sally Snaub, is that you? I would never have recognized you."

Actually, Sally hadn't changed since the last time she'd seen her a year ago. Juniper had managed to avoid her since then and Jack respectfully kept Sally away from their work sites. Her hair was the same shade of jet black, a voluminous cloud around her heart-shaped, perfectly made-up face and she still wore the same self-satisfied smirk. The same figure-hugging band-aid clothing that showcased her cavernous cleavage and screamed of desperation. Big brown eyes were adorned with spiky, black false lashes and her Cupid's bow mouth was painted with high gloss, red lipstick. She was attractive in a rather obvious way, and Juniper thought how much prettier the woman would look without all that makeup plastered on her face.

"Juniper, you haven't changed at all." Sally smiled, her eyes lighting up like a Christmas tree. "I just wanted to let you know how sorry I was to hear that you weren't modeling anymore. It is a shame," she said, clucking her tongue. "But that's the fashion industry for you. You turn thirty and gain a few pounds and it's all over. Oh well, you hide it well." Sally shook her head in pity.

Juniper smirked. "I'm twenty-eight and I stopped taking jobs to focus on the renovation business. But you're so lucky you've never had to worry about such things. It must be nice to gain as much weight as you want. I mean it's not like anyone cares to look at you. Oh well, at least you have Jack bagged."

Sally scowled. "And you have Jack's company to fall back on."

Juniper adjusted the headband in her short blonde hair. Time to hit below the belt. "You mean mine and Jack's company. I just love working with him. It's like we're still a couple. You must miss him—he spends so much time with me—I don't know how the two of you even find time together."

Sally stiffened and Juniper knew she'd hit her right in the sore spot. "Jack and I have never been happier. In fact, we are planning to tie the knot at last. I hope you can attend."

"Yes," Juniper said, looking over Sally's shoulder. "Why, there's the future groom. I think I'll go over and see how the rest of his day was. I haven't seen him in an hour. He might need a back rub… his shoulders were awfully tight from all that hammering today."

Sally stepped closer to Juniper. "You should really keep your hands to your own boyfriend. Oh, that's right. Jack told me your boyfriend broke it off." She shook her head sadly. "Pity."

Juniper flushed angrily. "I broke it off."

"Were you able to bring a date, at least?"

"There you are." A man reached for Juniper's hand. "How would you like to dance?"

Juniper breathed a sigh of relief as the man's left hand found her waist.

"I was afraid you weren't going to show up tonight," he whispered into her ear.

She leaned back so she could look up into his hazel eyes. "I almost didn't, but I'm really glad I did. I'm sorry, have we met?"

He smiled, his eyes crinkling up in the process. "No, but I know Pike and I've heard all about you. She's the one who sent me over. I'm Cody Lumos. I'm the new detective in town, that's why I was hoping you would be here. You know, outsiders stick together and all that."

"Well, thank you for rescuing me, Detective."

"I've never seen two people tear one another apart in such a condescending yet polite manner."

"You haven't been around many Victoria's Secret models then, have you?"

Cody laughed. "No, I'm afraid. I have not. A truly honed skill set I'm assuming. Have you two been friends long?"

Juniper tilted her head. "Do you know my business partner, Jack Young? He grew up here."

"Not very well, but sort of, I bought a house on Queen Street about a month ago. Jack Sr. was my real estate agent."

"Well the girl I was mincing words with is Jack's fiancée. She replaced me four years ago and we haven't really gotten along since then."

Cody smiled at her. "I can see why."

"Pike mentioned you and she are old college friends? Is that how you met Jack?"

"Yes. Pike and I were recruited on campus by the same modeling agency. Jack was taking the same building science course as me and he knew Pike. We were like the three musketeers during college and then Sally the shark showed up and practically stalked us. It didn't take long for her to sink her teeth into Jack once I was away modeling."

"Well, he's not a very intelligent guy to let her bite, but that's just my opinion," Cody added. "What about the Patone crew? How do you know them?"

"Through Jack and Pike. Anyway, it's more like who doesn't know them. They're Bohemian royalty. At least that's what they think. Pike and Kaitlyn have always been frenemies and now that they're working together on the Halloween Ball, things are especially strained."

"There you are," Kaitlyn said. "I've been waiting to see you."

Juniper looked up in surprise to hear Kaitlyn's voice. Hopefully she hadn't overheard them.

"Kaitlyn. I didn't see you there."

Kaitlyn hovered rudely. "Is it true?"

Juniper frowned. She had no idea what Kaitlyn was talking about and she wasn't about to volunteer anything.

"Did you see it?" Kaitlyn pressed.

"See what?"

"Did you see the ghost today?"

"Oh." Juniper nodded, finally grabbing a clue. "I don't know. I saw a woman in a white dress in the garden."

"That's it?"

"It all happened very fast. I don't know that it was a ghost or a prank, but there was some very creepy violin music playing. Your mother said you've seen her… have you heard the music as well?"

Kaitlyn snorted. "Of course, she'd tell you that." She rolled her eyes. "I have to go."

Cody shook his head, clearly confused. "Do you make enemies wherever you go?"

Frustrated, Juniper shook it off, "I have no idea what that was all about. Shall we go sit down? I see Pike."

Jack, who Juniper noticed had been glaring at them dancing, suddenly got to his feet. "I'll see everyone later. I've got an early morning."

Before Jack could completely leave the table, Sally said, "Excellent idea, honey, I'll be home shortly."

Jack frowned and walked away.

It didn't escape Juniper's notice that Jack didn't kiss Sally goodbye—trouble in the shark tank?

"Was it something I said?" Cody whispered into Juniper's ear.

Juniper's lips curved into a smile.

The party was in full swing now. Couples were swaying to the music. Almost every table was full. The food smelled delicious. Helen spared no expense on her parties.

"Is it true the Halloween Ball is at the old Doctor's place this year? I heard Jack Young bought it," a younger girl Juniper didn't recognize asked.

"It's true. Have you met Juniper?" Pike motioned in Juniper's direction. "She's Jack's partner."

"Business partner," Sally said, snidely.

"Business partner and ex-girlfriend," Pike clarified. "They were generous enough to agree to lend it for the night of the ball."

"Jack is hot! I used to have a crush on him when I was a kid. I'm Kingston," the girl said, sticking out her hand.

Sally stormed away with a huff.

"Here." One of the younger guys reached into his pocket, pulled out a bill, and laid it on the table. "I bet five dollars someone gets murdered the night of the ball."

"Oliver, what kind of thing is that to say," Helen said, turning up at the table.

Oliver looked up at the woman who'd just cuffed him in the ear. "Sorry, Aunt Helen, but you know what they say about that place and it's the one-hundred-year anniversary."

"You're such a dope," Axl teased, elbowing his younger cousin. He lowered his voice. "Who bets five bucks? You're so cheap."

"Sorry, I'm not rich like you," Oliver shot back, rubbing his ear.

"All right, enough bickering!" She wagged her finger. "And there will be no more talk about murder. You should see the feast the church ladies have prepared. Why don't you three go find the others and help carry things out?"

Axl groaned but got to his feet obediently, tugging at his cousin's collar. "Fine. Come on."

"If you'll excuse me. I'd better go supervise them," Helen said, turning.

"Supervise!" Pike snorted. "Heaven forbid, that woman lift a ruby red finger nail to help. She'd probably pass out from exhaustion."

"Speaking of which, I'm pretty tired myself. I think I'm going to head home now," Juniper said to Pike, forcing a yawn.

"No fricking way, Palmer! You stay here with me until the end. I need the moral support and perhaps some

physical restraint." Pike dropped her voice. "Pleeaasse…
Kaitlyn's near at hand and I don't want to be left alone with
her. She keeps texting me that we need to talk. I may be
known as the nice girl in Bohemian Lake, but one more
insult from her and I'm gonna choke her out, birthday party
or not."

FIVE

Juniper bolted upright in the haunted mansion's antique bed too quickly, wrenching her neck in the process. She rubbed the muscles with one hand trying to decipher just what in the heck had woken her.

Her pulse was going faster than Pike's pumpkin pie at a charity event.

She blinked, unsuccessfully trying to make out shadows in the dark room.

Nothing. There was nothing.

It was just her imagination, she soothed. She was just exhausted from working on the house all day, and then dealing with Jack's frosty girlfriend and the Patone dynasty, she'd gone to bed three hours after she'd intended to and had a nightmare.

Yes, that was it.

Slowly, she let out her breath, feeling some of the tension leave her shoulders and back. Her cellphone read, way too flipping early, also known as 5:35 a.m. She set it aside and rubbed her eyes. The thought that something more had disturbed her sleep still niggling at the back of her brain. Afterall, she didn't recall a nightmare. If anything, she'd been enjoying herself. She'd been having an interesting dream about a certain detective that she wanted to get back to. Of course, the detective had morphed into Jack.

The sound of rain pouring down the uncovered window pane and the loud clap of thunder clued her in to what might have woken her. Still exhausted, she brought the covers over her head and drifted back off. She and Jack normally took turns crashing at the houses they were flipping. Vacant houses invited problems.

She didn't know how long she lay there, half-asleep and half-awake, before a bang caused her to jump from the bed. She stood there in confusion, waiting for something more to happen. A noise. A shout. Something that would cue her into what she'd heard was real and not part of a nightmare. Several minutes passed without another sound. Surely, it was nothing more than a dream.

Shivering, Juniper walked over to the bedroom door and cracked it open. She had a great view of the hallway and the backyard outside through the tall stained-glass window. Might as well check things out. She pulled on her jeans and tugged a cream-colored sweater down over her tank top before creeping out and leaning over the railing. Had one of the boxes fallen over again? The bannister was glossy and cold to the touch and almost instantly sent shivers up the back of her neck. Or was that from something else—a sixth sense. She took the stairs one at a time until a shadow, seen from the corner of her eye, moved on the lower level. Last night's ghost tour flashed in her mind. Everything was so quiet and the gloomy light filtered in and flickered, making the tools that were piled on the floor below look like ominous instruments of death. She told herself that it was just the wind stirring the tree branches.

Six a.m. and Jack's return couldn't come fast enough. He was never later than that.

"Jack?" Juniper shouted.

No response.

Crrrrreeeeeaaaaaaakkkkkkk.

The sound of the loose step under her feet made her nervous but seeing that everything was still in place and Juniper was alone, she turned around and moved back up the stairs to the second floor. The paranoia pressed heavy against her and she couldn't resist a quick glimpse behind her. Big mistake. She caught sight of a dark-haired woman through the stained-glass window running across the yard in a flash of white.

Juniper's chest felt tight as she considered her next move. Her heart thumped in a crazy rhythm. She gauged the distance back to the bedroom where she'd left her cellphone, but who would she call, Ghostbusters? She launched into action, flying down the stairs and straight into something hard.

"Junie?"

Juniper jumped at the sound of her name.

A blinding flash of lightning followed by a shattering crack of thunder filled the foyer. Juniper blinked and attempted to adjust her eyes. She wrapped her arms around Jack and took a calming breath. Soft music emanated from the headphones that now hung around his neck and the front door was open. There were multiple bags inside the door.

Jack ticked an eyebrow upward in an exaggerated leer after she pulled back.

"You feelin' frisky, Palmer?"

Juniper opened her mouth to tell Jack what she'd just seen—what she'd thought she'd seen—but she snapped her jaws shut instead. No matter how hard she tried to come up with a logical explanation for what she'd just experienced.

There was no rational explanation. Maybe Juniper was having an honest-to-goodness nervous breakdown. That was it. She'd finally gone cuckoo.

"Sorry. That was inappropriate of me." Juniper straightened and Jack's arms fell away.

"Yes, workplace sexual harassment does seem to be a problem here. We'd best go see HR now." His whisky brown eyes sparkled and the lines around his eyes deepened. They'd spent so much their time keeping their emotions in check that Juniper cherished the moments they relaxed and joked like old times.

"I guess I walked into that one, huh?" Juniper laughed, patting at her hair. "I got spooked, but I'm okay. I'm gonna go get a coffee. Do you want anything?"

"Maybe, I'll come with you. Why don't we have breakfast together for a change?" Jack reached for his phone as it buzzed in his pocket. "Oh, just a sec. I have to take this." Juniper's grin faded and her mood nosedived when she saw it was Sally calling.

"Hey, Sal—" He held up his index finger in a motion for Juniper to wait a minute then he walked away.

Juniper sighed and left the house. Based on her sweaty palms and racing pulse, she still hadn't gotten over him. But there was no way, she was waiting around and playing second fiddle. She walked across the darkened road, trying to enjoy the crisp air and smell of fallen leaves. It wasn't raining yet, but it looked like it wanted to. She peeked through the glass of Pike's cafe. The sign said closed, but bakers, like construction workers were up at dawn. Pike was dressed in a gray and yellow apron and had her hair tucked into a white frilly cap. "It's open."

The aroma of pumpkin wafted through the open door.

"Ready for some coffee?" Pike asked.

"Yes please… extra strong." A timer rang from the back, "Help yourself."

Juniper poured a steaming hot cup and followed her into a backroom prep space that was messy with baking ingredients, bowls, and a mixer on the counter.

"Smells delicious," she said as Pike pulled three pies out of the oven and put them on cooling racks.

"So, how was your first night in the haunted mansion?"

Juniper took a sip from her coffee and said nothing.

"I knew it!" Pike turned and wiped her hands on a towel. "You saw the ghost of Victoria again, didn't you?"

Juniper just stood there.

"Sooner or later you're going to have to tell me," Pike said as she rolled out some dough for another pie.

"And why is that?"

"Because I'm your friend. And I won't make fun of you or think you're crazy for having seen ghosts. Or… whatever it was you saw, or experienced. Not that I'm saying you have, you know. Just in case you did."

Juniper shrugged and toyed with the handle of her mug. She preferred to play her cards close to her chest but Pike was her best friend. Finally, she opened her mouth to say something and her stomach growled. "Oops. Apparently, you have to feed me if you want me to talk."

"Right. I'm a terrible hostess. I've got fresh apple strudel, chocolate croissants and raspberry-chai doughnuts this morning."

Juniper reached for the apple strudel, which was still so hot she could barely touch it. "What time were you up at? You could run the world, woman, with all you accomplish in a day."

Pike rolled her eyes as she handed Juniper a fork. "Well, the first wave starts rolling in at 6:00 a.m. so if there aren't fresh baked goods then there's hell to pay." She began to unload the tray of doughnuts into one of the glass cases that would later be transported to the front counter. "Which reminds me, you now have ten minutes to spill what's bothering you before we're rushed by grumpy old men wishing to discuss their latest ailment—everything from sleep problems to prostate trouble."

"Please—I'm trying to eat!" Juniper shuddered, setting her fork down. The strudel was still too hot for the moment.

"I'm just saying… you're running out of time."

"Yes, okay. I may have gotten a little spooked this morning," Juniper admitted, licking the apple from her fingers, "Jack came over early and he startled me."

Pike made a gushing noise. Her eyes lit up. "He still loves you! Told you so," she made a face. "You need to steal him back."

"Holy, jump to conclusions much. He just worries about our project houses getting broken into and sometimes he switches up his hours so that we're not as predictable," Juniper uncrossed her legs and pushed herself away from the counter. "We're business partners and friends. That's it. It's been four years and, in case you forgot, he's planning to marry that witch."

Pike reached out and pulled Juniper back down. "The fact that you still hate her tells me you care."

"Nonsense, I just don't like how controlling she is."

"Controlling, because she doesn't want him spending all his time with you?" She flung her hand out, gesturing from Juniper's head to her toes. "Have you looked in a mirror girl? No woman would want her man hanging out with you all day and night."

"Well, for one thing, he's my ex, and things obviously didn't work out for a reason, and two, we're in business together, so she needs to deal with it."

Pike snorted. "Or you could just put her out of her misery by taking him back."

Juniper looked at her friend and smiled. You had to love the girl's persistence.

"Anyway, his coming into the house combined with the storm startled me from my sleep and in my heightened state of wimpy-ness, I kind of sort of, saw the ghost again, or at least I think I did."

Pike put down her croissant and leaned in until she was clutching Juniper's arm. "You think you did?"

Juniper nodded. "She was running."

Juniper heard someone let out a little gasp that sounded like air leaving a balloon. The girls both walked out front.

"Lulu?" Pike said.

Juniper frowned. "Huh?" She swung her gaze to the front door, even as Pike darted toward it. Lulu stood in the door frame, arms juggling several stacks of boxes.

"You gonna move all your stuff in? I don't think we can fit another dresser," Pike joked.

Lulu looked like she was going to cry. She hurried into the back with Pike in tow.

Juniper saw that as her cue to take off. She didn't want to get into anyone else's business. This town knew far too much about what was going on with one another as it was. "I'm just gonna take some treats for the crew. I'll leave the money under the cash register," Juniper bellowed hoping Pike could hear her.

She had just gotten a box full of doughnuts ready and a tray of coffee when in walked the detective, flanked by a sour looking Helen and her son, Axl.

"Juniper, I'm glad we ran in to you. Have you seen Kaitlyn?" Helen bit her lip. She looked genuinely upset.

Juniper looked around the store. "Not since yesterday."

She was just about to leave when Pike rounded the corner. "Detective Lumos, I made your favorite Danish."

"Thanks, Pike," The Detective looked down, "but I'm here with Helen and I'm on duty. I don't suppose you've seen Kaitlyn yet?"

"Nope, not yet."

A worried look crossed his face. "We were hoping she'd be back by now. She didn't come home last night."

Helen took a step forward, pointing a finger at Pike, "And we know the two of you had a fight yesterday."

The detective glanced over at Helen. "Why don't you wait outside? You're distraught."

"We did have an argument yesterday, but it was nothing heated," Pike retorted.

"That's not what we heard," Helen sniped back.

Juniper felt the need to diffuse the situation. "Look. Isn't it possible she spent the night at her boyfriends? It was Saturday." She smiled brightly and ran her hand through her hair. Detective Lumos looked good this morning, and she looked… well she hadn't even checked to see how she looked. Maybe Pike was right, and she needed to put some effort into her appearance.

"She doesn't have a boyfriend," Helen hissed.

"Well I saw her getting into a red sports car on Friday."

Lulu rounded the corner, still looking disheveled.

"Lulu, does Peter still drive that red Camaro?" Helen asked.

"Yes. Why?"

Juniper shook her head. She could see where this was going. "I'll see you guys later. I've got to get back over to the house."

"I'll be right behind you," Pike said. "Sarah gets in for her shift in five minutes."

The house was bustling with activity when Juniper returned with coffee and doughnuts for the volunteers. Jack was on a ladder polishing the huge chandelier that hung from the ceiling, its crystals reflecting a rainbow of colors from the foyer's double entry stained glass windows.

"Hey Slacker! Nice to see you back."

"Oh Jack, that looks amazing, but you make me so nervous."

"I'm fine. Don't worry."

Juniper set down the coffee and treats and motioned upstairs. "Is Kaitlyn here?"

"What? Why would she be here this early? Princess only stops by in the evenings to point out all of our faults."

Juniper shook her head. "She didn't go home last night and mommy dearest is not happy."

"Uh-oh? She's sure to get the credit card taken away for that one."

Juniper chuckled, carefully passing by him to reach the second floor. Jack always knew how to make her laugh. "Well, at least the town's finest takes missing adults seriously. That way if this ghost gets me tonight… you won't have to wait forty-eight hours to report it."

"I'll protect you," Pike said, suddenly appearing at the bottom of the stairs.

"That was quick!"

"Yeah, I had to get out of there or be arrested for assaulting Helen."

Pike and Juniper entered the narrow staircase and trotted up the steps that led to the third-floor attic space.

Juniper paused at the top to open the door and saw something out of the corner of her eye in one of the old servant's quarters.

"What is it?" Pike asked, practically bumping into her.

"Someone's been here. There's a wine bottle on its side that wasn't there yesterday." Juniper did a double take. There was also a sleeping bag and a candle in the corner on top of the Oriental rug.

A scratching sound came from the main attic where they'd been working yesterday.

Pike pushed passed her as if she heard it too.

"Did that trunk just bark?" Juniper asked, confused.

"That has to be our imagination—either that or it's the ghost of our dear doctor's wife."

"I don't think ghosts bark," Juniper said crossing the room.

"Last one!" Axl called out as he carried a box up the stairs. "Need anything else up here?"

"Liquid courage." Pike retorted.

"Um…" Axl walked back towards the stairs. "Sure. I'll see what I can do."

Get a grip, Juniper told herself as she lifted the lid of the trunk. Her nose twitched at the smell and then she realized why.

Curled up inside, eyes vacant and fixed like the dummy on the floor, was a body. The little dog that had been closed in with the corpse began to bark.

SIX

"My sister! Oh God, it's my sister, Kaitlyn." The dog sprung from the trunk and ran behind Juniper to where Axl stood with tears in his eyes. Behind him were some of the other volunteers.

Juniper stood for a moment and willed her heart to stop racing. She pulled him tight to her chest. His ragged breathing filled her ears, and the little dog trembled between them. Finally, she spoke to the room. "Okay, everyone, listen. We're going to go back outside and…"

She realized Pike was already heading down the steps, a phone to her ear, speaking to a police dispatcher. Thank goodness someone was on the ball.

"Pike's calling the police. Come on, Axl, we don't want to contaminate anything."

She turned to usher the gang out, but Axl pushed past her and went to kneel beside the trunk that held his sister's body. He set the dog aside and reached his hand in.

"Axl, no!" Juniper said, softening her voice. "You can't touch her yet, okay?"

"She's dead," Axl whispered.

Juniper put a hand on his shoulder and, as gently as she could, urged him to come with her.

"Who could have done this!" wailed one of the girls.

"Please. We have to get her out of the trunk. She looks uncomfortable," Axl pleaded.

"We can't touch her. There could be evidence," Juniper rationalized.

"Oh, God. I could have saved her!" Axl cried. "She called me from here around seven asking if I'd give her a ride home. Only I had a date, so I'd already left and she was here by herself… and now she's dead! Kaitlyn! I'm sorry."

"You can't think like that, Axl," Juniper said, wrapping her arm around his shoulders and leading him down the stairs.

"I don't feel so good," Axl muffled as they got into the front entry hall.

"It's okay. We're almost outside. You just need some fresh—" She jumped back just in time.

The little dog in his arms was not so lucky.

"It's okay," she soothed as she tugged him and the dog out the main door. "Come on, Axl. Someone else will clean that up later."

Still with the phone at her ear, apparently on hold, Pike stood and urged the group out onto the porch.

Juniper gave an initial statement to the first policeman on the scene and then waited on the porch while they checked out the scene. The forensics team had arrived by that point and was combing the Doctor's House for evidence.

With the volunteers clustered outside, she walked to the road and took in huge gulps of air. The stench of death had been so strong she felt like she could still taste it or maybe that was just her imagination working overtime. Between the dizziness and the pounding in her ears, she suddenly wished for something to lean against.

Small houses lined the road, with curious neighbors lingering out front of them. It was the kind of neighborhood, where people knew one another, where you hung laundry on the line and chatted with whoever passed by, where you would find packs of kids playing games in the street—not the kind of place where you found dead bodies.

It only took a few steps for Jack to reach her side. He lightly touched her elbow and called her name. On a normal day, she would have immediately smiled, and turned her full attention to him. Today was not a normal day.

He gripped her arm harder. "Junie, look at me," he demanded.

"Did you see anyone in there? Besides the volunteers."

"No."

"I'm so glad you weren't hurt." He put his other hand on her shoulder and pulled her in for a hug. It had been a while since Jack hugged her and this was twice in one day. It felt way too good. She pulled away but allowed him to hold her hand.

Pandemonium was breaking out by the minute. The lawn and street were slowly flooding with neighbors. Not to mention, the neighbor had hosed the little dog off and wrapped him in a towel but he'd gotten loose and was now running around the lawn with officers falling all over themselves trying to catch him.

Some poor young policeman was trying to take control and get everyone to go back to their homes and stores. Unfortunately, everyone was talking at once and no one was listening.

Juniper looked over her shoulder and saw Helen approaching her and Jack, just as the dog ran up to them barking its little head off. He pawed at Juniper's leg like he wanted up but when she bent to scoop him, he looked back over his shoulder and got spooked, growling, and darting away.

"I'm so sorry, Helen," Juniper whispered, wrapping her free arm around the older woman. Jack hung steadfast to Juniper's hand, realizing she still needed the support.

For once Helen was speechless. She wasn't even crying—she just wordlessly shook her head like she was in shock.

"Where's Frank? Helen? Someone needs to find Frank," Juniper said, speaking calmly.

"I'll do it," Jack said, finally letting go of Juniper's hand.

Helen nodded her head and allowed a medical attendant to place a blanket around her shoulders and steer her away.

Juniper took the opportunity to find Pike, and they watched as Detective Lumos came out of the house, taking control of the growing mob. Clearly things like this didn't happen every day in this sleepy little town.

Exasperated, the detective shouted, "I want everyone's attention. Everyone and I mean everyone, who does not belong here needs to go home or back to work now. Anyone who was on the property before or during the discovery has to stay. Stay out of the way but no one is to leave the area. Does everyone understand? Good. Get going."

At that moment, Lulu appeared. Her face was pink and her breathing rapid as she pushed through the crowd. "What's going on? Why are these people out front?"

Pike looked at her sympathetically. "Oh, Lulu–I'm sorry—there's been an accident. Um, perhaps, we should take you to Helen."

"Will someone please tell me what's going on?" Lulu's voice had risen to a panicked screech. "Oh my God! Has something happened to Peter? Let me get on—I need to see him. Is he OK?"

"It's not your husband, Mrs. McCloskey." Detective Lumos was authoritative, but gentle in his tone. "It's your niece," he said as he looked at his notebook. "I'm afraid she's dead."

Juniper watched as Lulu's face crumpled and she began to cry—great, shaking sobs that came from deep inside.

After a few minutes, Lulu's weeping subsided. "Oh, I'm sorry… I just can't believe it," she said, as she wiped her eyes and blew her nose, "The ghost got her. I warned her not to go in there. Why doesn't anyone ever listen to me?"

"Lulu! Lulu! What the bloody hell's going on?" a deep voice shouted from across the lawn as a tall man with dark, slicked-back hair walked towards them.

"Oh, Peter—she's dead. The ghost killed her just like I warned you. That place should never have been sold." Lulu clung to him as she cried.

"What? Who's dead?" He tried to shove his way past Detective Lumos, but was stopped.

"Kaitlyn," Lulu whispered as she tugged at his arm. "Kaitlyn's dead. They found her body in the trunk in the attic."

"Dead? What do you mean, dead? How did she die?"

"We don't know yet," Detective Lumos said, taking charge. "The coroner will be arriving soon to remove the body and ascertain the cause of death. At the moment, we have reason to believe that there are suspicious circumstances, so until we've established the facts, I'm afraid no one is allowed back in the Mansion. We're treating the attic as a potential crime scene until we know more. Now if you'll excuse me." He turned and began speaking to another officer.

"Come on," Pike said kindly. "Let's go back to the café. I'll make you a cup of coffee or tea, and some breakfast, if you like."

"You're not supposed to leave," Juniper whispered.

"The Detective knows where to find me."

Juniper nodded and watched Pike lead the distraught couple away. After that she headed in the opposite direction following the brick herringbone pathway that looped around the house. Jack was up on the hill sitting on the bench that overlooked the house. As she wandered toward him, she glanced back at the damaged window frames, cracked brick, a mossy roof—it all contributed to the house's eerie Gothic air. In less than a week from now this place was supposed to host a Haunted Halloween Ball to raise funds for the historical society but there would be no Halloween party at the Doctor's House this year. Not after something like this.

Juniper let out a whoosh of air as she sat down beside him. She hadn't known Kaitlyn well, but she hadn't really liked her and now there was guilt gnawing at her insides. "Did I really just find Kaitlyn Patone's dead body? And in our house."

The manor's signs of neglect did little to distance her from the memory of Kaitlyn's folded up body.

Jack leaned back and rubbed the dark stubble on his jaw. "Oh, babe," he said, resorting to an old term of endearment. His voice quiet as they sat side-by-side and gazed up at the Gothic square tower, topped by the imposing iron widow's walk; it looked stark against the bright gray sky.

"It really is a haunted house now, right? Not one death here, but three?" Juniper responded.

They were used to vehicles parked in their driveways—plumbers, electricians, carpenters, inspectors—but this was the first time they'd had multiple police cars.

Two stern looking officers were unspooling crime tape around the house. The tape fluttered in the brisk breeze, the yellow practically glowing against the red brick.

"The entire house?" Juniper said, watching from the bench. "They're going to wrap the entire house in crime scene tape?"

Jack patted her leg. "Like a giant present that no one wants."

"And everyone in town will know," Juniper said, shaking her head.

"Uh, pretty sure the cat is out of the bag. Have you seen the driveway."

He was right, of course. The Doctor's house was now the busiest place on the street—and it was located across from Cookies & Corsets Café where everyone hung out.

Juniper sighed. "This is not how I envisioned things going." He put his arm around her and she leaned into his side. His body felt good. Solid. Reassuring.

"I know and not to be insensitive or anything, but… if word of this gets out, we are never going to flip this house."

"Tell me about it. By the way, did you get a hold of Frank Patone?"

"No answer. I spoke to his secretary though, and she said she was going to get word to him ASAP to call Helen." He replied.

Glancing down the hill at the back door of the house, Juniper saw Axl and his mom crying and holding each other.

The volunteers had broken away. She'd overheard Helen repeating to the detective what a nice girl Kaitlyn had been. Who would have done this to her? Was it a break-in gone wrong?

Juniper couldn't help but think that Helen was delusional. Kaitlyn had made plenty of enemies, and yet, had someone really killed her?

Two of the volunteers had separated and were now walking in their direction. They heard one of them say, "I bet the Halloween ball will, like, totally sell out."

Juniper was still leaning into Jack and felt him go very stiff. Her own shoulders slumped as she imagined their plans for this house and the future dissolve. Those kids were wrong, there was no way the Patone family and the town of Bohemian Lake would allow this ball to go on now. And there was no way they'd sell it.

SEVEN

Anyway, if you're making coffee, I'll have one too, please, but can you put it in a takeaway cup, and can I get a slice of that lemon meringue I smell cooling." Detective Lumos sat back and stretched out his long legs. Juniper thought he looked tired.

"So, I guess it wasn't natural causes, huh?" Harold asked as he sipped a creamy vanilla bean coffee through a pillow of foam.

"Uncle Harold, you know I can't tell you anything," Detective Lumos scolded.

"I'm just saying, Kaitlyn was rather young to have just dropped dead, don't you think?"

"Well, even young people die. You should take a hint." The Detective took a sip from his plastic cup and cursed under his breath as he scalded his tongue.

"Mind yourself, nephew. You might be big, but I can still whack you with my cane."

Juniper smirked.

"Besides, I hardly think the lass folded herself up in a trunk."

Detective Lumos shifted uncomfortably. "Can we just drop this subject? We won't know for sure until the coroner's report comes back." His phone rang, interrupting him. "Yes, OK, I'll be right there." He stood up to leave and lowered his voice. "I have to go."

Pike shuddered. "Your slice of pie will be waiting."

"Thanks, hopefully I can get back before you close."

"See you then," Juniper said.

"That you will," he smiled briefly and winked, before striding out the door.

"Did he just wink at you?" Pike could barely contain herself. "I think our new Detective is sweet on you. What do you think, Harold? Maybe Juniper should ask him out?" she nudged Juniper mischievously.

"Will you please STOP trying to push me at every man that crosses my path? Yesterday it was poor Jack, and today it's Lumos."

"They're bringing out the body now," Harold interrupted their silly banter.

Juniper shuddered involuntarily as a stretcher carrying Kaitlyn in a dark blue body bag passed by. She noticed that some of the assembled crowd were taking pictures and videos on their phones. She'd barely known Kaitlyn, but no one deserved such disrespect.

"Honestly, it's a good thing that Peter took Lulu home. The behavior of some people is just unbelievable, isn't it?" Juniper said.

"It's just morbid curiosity," Pike replied. "People can't help themselves." She drank the last of her coffee and washed up her cup. "I guess that means you'll be able to go back inside again soon."

"Yeah, lucky me."

"Hey," Pike said, reaching out to touch Juniper's arm. "You know you can stay with me for as long as you need, right?"

Juniper cast her mind back to the scene in the attic. There hadn't been blood or anything messy. But those eyes, just staring up at her, they would haunt her forever.

"I think I will, Pike, sleep at your place for a while, that is. Thank you."

EIGHT

S parkling despite the gloomy weather, the stained glass windows of the church on the hill had a certain charm that bested the cemetery's looming gray clouds.

"Ashes to ashes, dust to dust; looking for the resurrection of the dead, and the life of the world to come, through our Lord Jesus..." The Pastor's voice was somber in the presence of the assembled mourners.

As Kaitlyn was laid to rest, the tears streamed down many of the townspeople's cheeks, but most surprising was Peter McCloskey. Lulu clung to her husband, practically hysterical, and on the other side of her looking a little more stoic, was Helen and Frank and their remaining two children Axl and Meaghen.

Approaching the coffin, Peter placed a single white rose on its lid. "I'm sorry," he whispered, before practically fleeing the scene. Lulu who was clad in all black was half dragged as she clung to his arm.

Pike leaned into Juniper under the oversized red umbrella they shared with Eve and whispered, "As if losing her niece wasn't bad enough, Lulu has to put up with his bizarre behavior."

"Aunt Lulu… Uncle Peter! Wait!" Meg called, her heels sinking into the sodden earth as she chased after them.

"Sorry for the scene," Helen sniffed as they approached the coffin to say their goodbyes. "My cousin and her husband have the tendency to make everything about them."

Pike shot what Juniper knew was a look of displeasure. Pike was fiercely loyal to Lulu and from everything Juniper knew, the comment didn't fit. Lulu was a sweet, thoughtful person who never wanted attention for herself.

A strong gust of wind took hold of Eve's umbrella, thrashing it against their faces. "Time to get out of this rain, I think," Juniper whispered as she patted Pike's arm. The rain was coming in sideways now.

A 'Celebration of Life' was being held for Kaitlyn at Fern Baron's house, and they'd hired Pike to cater the food. Pike and Juniper had dropped the sandwiches off before the service but there were a few things they needed to pick up from Cookies & Corsets.

As Pike opened the doors to the café, Juniper felt her spirits lift. Pike's assistant was behind the counter pouring coffee. Harold, his nephew Detective Lumos, and Jack Sr., were all there, dressed in suits, at one of the tables, sipping from Pike's signature yellow polka-dot porcelain mugs. The room held the blended aroma of fresh-brewed coffee, cinnamon, and sugar. It was like coming home after a long day. The familiar faces of the Cookies & Corsets regulars were beginning to represent solace and security. Juniper had never felt this way in any other place, not even the city she'd grown up in, but there was no time to dwell on that now. People were expected to arrive at Fern's place across the road at any moment, and Juniper and Pike needed to get there to complete the set up.

"First thing ... let's get out of these heels," Pike said.

Juniper was glad that they'd thought to leave a couple of pairs of ballet flats at the café that morning. She was not used to traipsing about on heels thinner than the nails she hammered.

In the backroom, Juniper checked herself in the mirror. Her eyeliner was smeared, and her bob, the color of white sugar was plastered to her face. Towel-drying her hair briskly, she ran her fingers through it and pulled it up into a half top-knot. Then, using a makeup wipe and some oil, she cleaned up underneath her eye.

Re-appraising her reflection, she felt happier with the face that looked back at her. Her eyes were clear now and her hair looked much less like she'd been dragged through a hedge. Slicking a wand of rose-gold gloss across her full lips and dusting the lightest covering of bronzer onto her cheeks, she nodded at the mirror.

Five minutes later, she and Pike were across the road carrying the last of the baked goods. Thankfully, the rain had paused for the moment. Pike's employee had brewed the coffee and set all the food up along the buffet hutch.

"It's on days like this that I'm thankful we've got such a close-knit community," Pike said as she sent one of the helpers across the road for another tray. "It's like having ten extra sets of hands."

"Hmmm," Juniper said, distracted, as she took the tinfoil off the dishes. Pickled egg salad on a croissant (the café's specialty), grilled chicken, apple and gouda, and a slow cooker of slowly bubbling cream of potato soup, two dishes of apple crisp with a jug of apple cider, and two huge trays of raisin butter tarts were among the buffet selection. "I hope there'll be enough for everyone."

"Enough?!" exclaimed Juniper. "Good grief, woman! There's enough here to feed the whole town for a week! This is the most extravagant funeral faire I've ever had."

Pike relaxed a little. "I'm glad you think so. Helen would have a fit if it weren't."

"Did someone say something about raisin tarts?" A voice from behind interrupted their conversation, and they turned to see Jack Sr. coming through Fern's front door with a whole posse of people.

"I might have guessed you'd be here first," Pike teased. "Worried you'd miss the sweet treats, were you?"

"Worried I'd miss you sweet young things, more like," retorted Jack Sr., his crow's feet gathered at the outer parts of his eye as he broke into a wide grin.

Harold's wife, Joanne, and her best friend, Eve, herded in last in bright yellow, plastic, hooded ponchos.

"Quit flirting, Jackie boy. You'd have a heart attack if one of them even blew you a kiss," Eve said as she hung her poncho on the coat rack and smoothed her hand over her chignon. "Perfect funeral weather, wouldn't you agree? I

COOKIES, CORPSES AND THE DEADLY HAUNT

hope it rains at my funeral… can't have anyone happy that day. Just wouldn't be right."

Juniper chuckled and nodded.

"Thank goodness it's such a short walk. Shove a cheek, boys, unless you'd prefer us to sit on your laps."

Harold and Jack Sr. did as they were told and shuffled down the dining room table's bench seating and the ladies were making themselves comfortable when Pike's Aunt Clara arrived. She was a frail-looking, softly spoken woman with a blue rinse and bright blue eyes. "Hello, everyone," Clara said as she stepped inside. "Is there room for one more?"

Pike and Juniper took turns greeting her. She'd buried her own husband the year before. Anticipating Clara being on the verge of tears, Joanne said loudly, "Did anyone else notice the drama happening at the church?" She ran some red lipstick over her mouth. "Was it just me, or was there some underlying tension happening between Peter and Helen?" She blotted her lips on a tissue before snapping her handbag shut. "I mean, Peter gritted his teeth all the way through the service, and then to take off like that, before everyone had said their goodbyes. Strange behavior, I thought."

"Yes, and of course Helen couldn't wait to blame Lulu for the scene," Pike said, her brow creased and her jade green eyes flashing with anger as she recalled Helen's words. "I'm lucky I had Juniper there to drag me away before I said something I regretted."

"Really? I didn't notice anything," Harold said.

"That's 'cause you'd already left." Joanne pointed out.

"Well, grief is a funny thing, isn't it," Eve said. "Everyone deals with it differently. Our most honorable Mayor for example—most fathers break down at the gravesite of their little girls. Such an unnatural thing—to lose a child—and yet I didn't even see that man shed a tear. I think he showed more emotion when he won the election."

"I remember Kaitlyn when she was growing up," Joanne said. "She was never particularly close to her parents, always seemed to be with Peter and Lulu. Of course, things changed when she became a teenager, she pulled away from the whole lot of them."

"Good grief!" The doors opened again and in walked Sally, with her parents and Jack in tow. "That rain is coming down by the bucket load now, and the wind is really starting to howl."

On seeing Jack's handsome face, Juniper immediately felt happier.

"Get ready for the onslaught?" said Jack, hungrily eyeing the food over Juniper's shoulder as he gave her a hug. "They'll be arriving any minute now," he said, moving into the next room to hug the older ladies.

The sound of cursing on the footpath that ran alongside the kitchen prompted Juniper to turn and look out of the open window. It was raining, but they had cracked the window when the caramel sauce for one of the cakes had burned.

"Bloody hell!" the voice repeated.

Juniper looked around the kitchen to see if there was anyone else bearing witness to the fact that Helen was standing with Lulu's husband, Peter, under a gazebo in the garden. *What are they doing out there?*

Juniper watched as Helen pushed Peter away—breaking into tears as she did. Not to be nosy but Juniper couldn't resist. She cracked the window an inch higher, doing so as quietly as possible.

They were far enough away that it was hard to hear but she couldn't miss when Helen slapped Peter hard across the face. Peter's eyes darted around and then shot to the house.

"Shoot!" Juniper ducked, but she was sure they'd seen her. That was her cue to get back to work. She slowly stood up and walked to the fridge—pretending to need something from it. She could hear footsteps coming back for the kitchen.

"Who were you talking to?" Pike asked, her head appearing in the doorway.

"It's you… you scared me half to death."

Pike gave her a worried look.

"Helen just slapped Peter in the gardens," Juniper said.

"What? Why?"

"I couldn't hear what she was saying but I'm sure she said Kaitlyn's name. Do you think Kaitlyn and Peter were having an affair?"

"Lulu's Peter? He's way too old for her. Not to mention he's her family."

"Wouldn't be the first time some middle-aged man has had an identity crisis and went after a young woman." Juniper pointed out.

"Yeah, but his niece?" Pike questioned.

"Well, she's technically not his niece. Helen and Lulu are cousins and Peter's not a blood relative."

"Right. I guess it wouldn't be the first time something like that has happened."

"I mean I did see her getting into a red sports car before she went missing, and Peter owns a red Camaro."

"True, and Peter looked unhinged this morning at the funeral—maybe it's guilt. Do you think Helen found out about the affair and confronted him?"

"Actually, I think she accused him of more than just that—I heard her call him a murderer."

"Peter is a hot head and I could see him being a worthless cheating son of a gun... but a killer?" She shrugged. "I just don't know."

Juniper glanced out the window just in time.

"Shhh, here they come."

A petite, but feisty Helen battled a large umbrella that had turned inside out as she returned to the pathway outside the kitchen. She cursed and gave up on the umbrella, finally pulling her jacket over her head. "Frank, Axl, are you two coming or what? I'm getting soaked!" Two adults and two teenagers appeared to catch up, running to get out of the rain as quickly as they could.

With Helen Patone leading the way, Kaitlyn's family stampeded through the French doors of the kitchen, quickly shedding their raincoats and boots.

"Pike, can you grab us some towels from the linen closet?"

"It's so nice to see you again, Juniper," Helen Patone said, her voice softening as she took the towel from Pike's hands and dried off. "Thank you for putting this all together."

"Well, it was actually Pike. I just assisted."

"Of course."

"Everything looks and smells delicious," Axl said, swiping a butter tart.

"Axl, where are your manners? You're dripping on the floor. Dry off and get a plate."

The girl who appeared at his side looked familiar to Juniper. "Hello, again. We've met before, right? You run the haunted tour?"

The girl nodded. "I'm Pearl."

"Yes." Juniper shook her hand. "I'm Juniper."

"Oh right. I forget sometimes that you don't know everyone," Helen said. "The past two weeks have all blurred together. One-minute Kaitlyn was here and the next she was gone. Anyway, there I go rambling again." She paused, as if to collect her thoughts. "Pearl was one of Kaitlyn's closest friends."

"Yes, come to think of it, the realtor, Jared Mitchell mentioned that when I toured the house. He said it was your idea to sell the house, Pearl, that you can see spirits or something, right?"

Helen blanched and Juniper realized the topic was clearly taboo. Before Juniper knew it Axl had swept the girl away into the next room. Meanwhile, Frank and Pike had disappeared to set up an extra table in the main room where people were gathering. Helen gently took Juniper's arm and walked her to the sink. "I need to ask a favor of you."

"Okay." Juniper was waiting for the words, *stop spying* to come from her perfectly lined red lips but instead Helen took a deep breath. "Kaitlyn told her father and I all about the Halloween project, she really loved that old house. I guess it's only fitting that she–well you know." Helen began to cry.

"I'm so sorry for your loss, Mrs. Patone. This has got to be hard."

"Please, call me Helen."

"Can I get you a drink or something to eat? We don't have to talk about any of this."

"No. I'm fine. I need to talk to someone and I'm not ready to face the main room yet." She dabbed at her eyes with a Kleenex.

Juniper cleared her throat. She found it odd that Helen was confiding in her. They barely knew each other.

"You said you needed a favor? How can I help you?"

"Oh right, yes, it's just Frank is insisting that we continue on with the ball in Kaitlyn's memory."

"Really?"

"Well now, don't be so shocked. We're not heartless people. It's just she was so devoted to this project and the historical society needs the money. I'm a touch more sensitive about it but Frank is right—it's just all so fresh to think about. Anyway, I was hoping I could come to the house next week or sometime before the fundraiser because… well, frankly, I could use some closure."

"You want to come to the Doctor's House?"

"Yes. I don't want the first time I step foot in the place to be the night of the ball. I'm afraid I'll make a scene, and, well, that just wouldn't do, now, would it?

"I understand. Of course. Anytime."

"Great. I'll pop by next week then." She dabbed at her eyes some more and then presto—the mask was back in place. Calm and composed Helen was ready to face the crowd.

NINE

J uniper looked around the kitchen and felt a ripple of excitement and fear run through her. The place was really coming together. The new cabinets and island had all been installed and the marble countertops were due to arrive today. They'd paid a pretty penny but this was high-end and they were going to get a pretty penny when they sold—if the place sold.

But did she really want to sell?

Doubt crept around her thoughts like one of the mansion's spiders as it had since they'd bought the old place. She shook her head and pushed the negative thoughts aside. She'd mulled over this and little else for the past couple of weeks. She had no choice. It was time. Every house they'd flipped for the past five years had been about getting to this moment. This house would give them the money they needed to go their own way. Jack could take the business and Juniper would do….

Well… anything she wanted.

She smiled. That was more like it.

Now all she needed was her painting overalls and she could put some lipstick on this baby.

She walked down the hall to the foyer and cast a critical eye up the wall. It was a good-sized room, and it would take a lot of paint.

Her paintbrushes were upstairs in the attic. For some reason, her pulse raced as she climbed the staircase to the second floor and entered the narrow staircase to the attic. The house just seemed unusually quiet. Every creak and groan of the old floorboards set her heart skittering. Juniper was used to being alone, but she felt a weight in the pit of her stomach, wishing Pike was with her.

She glanced inside the servants' quarters and noticed the threadbare Oriental rug and wine bottle had been taken as evidence. Something tingled at the back of her neck.

She whirled around, half expecting to see a ghost.

"Hello?" She ventured. "Anybody there?"

A horn sounded out front and she jumped, then immediately grew frustrated with herself for being so touchy.

You're in a small town. There's going to be lots of pop-in visitors.

She headed to the front window and saw Helen Patone making her way up the front walk.

Juniper frowned. She'd forgotten Helen had mentioned stopping by. Helen looked different today, her perfectly coiffed hair was down and messy and she constantly looked behind her in a nervous manner.

"Helen?" Juniper said, opening the door.

"Can I come in?"

Juniper hesitated a second before answering. "Yes. Of course. Is everything alright?"

"I, uh… not really. I need to talk to someone."

"Come on in," Juniper said.

Juniper started to bring up yesterday's conversation, but then she took a closer look at Helen. Her hand on the doorknob shook, and with her other hand, she pulled at the bottom of her blouse. Two threads stuck out and the hem in one spot sagged a tiny bit. Her skin, while pale naturally, wasn't only naturally pale right now. It was almost blanched.

Helen was scared.

"No problem," Juniper said. "Follow me. There's a couch in the parlor."

Helen hesitated a second, then stepped inside, closing the door behind her. She followed Juniper into the parlor and took a seat at the end of the couch where Juniper indicated. "This place is just as beautiful as I remember."

Juniper noticed one hand sneaking over a pendant that hung around her neck, most likely a cross or symbol of Christ. At least she had her faith, Juniper thought. That had to help at a time like this.

"You've been inside before?"

"Yes. My cousin Lulu used to own the house."

"I didn't realize that. The name on the real estate contract was different, Lucinda Atherton, I think."

"Her maiden name. Lulu is a nickname."

"Why didn't they live in it?"

"Lulu couldn't bear the ghosts." She looked over at Juniper. "She was always, how should I say it… sensitive."

"You've seen the ghosts?" Juniper asked.

"I've never seen them but it's always intrigued me. Our ancestors lived here—the Doctor and his wife."

"You were related to them? I didn't think from the story that they had time to have kids?"

"No. They didn't but Victoria's sister did. We don't broadcast it because it's not a very nice stigma to live with. By the way, my husband has decided that we will match funds to whatever the event raises." She looked thoughtful.

"That's a lovely gesture. I have to admit I was a little surprised to hear that you wanted to continue with the ball. I guess I assumed you'd call off the Halloween fundraiser, given what happened."

"My husband is a determined man."

"Can I get you a cup of coffee? There isn't much here by way of food but I always make sure the coffee is up and running when I'm working," Juniper said as she grabbed her Cookies & Corsets takeaway cup. "Of course, I often rely on the bakery across the road."

"That's okay," Helen said. "I'm too nervous to drink anything. I guess you noticed."

Juniper reached out and patted the woman's hand. "You can tell me anything," she said, repeating the words Jack always used when she was upset. "Would you prefer that we go back outside? We can talk on the porch or we can go across the street."

After a long moment, she nodded and said, "I'd rather stay here. Actually, can we go upstairs?" Helen got to her feet and faced Juniper. "I need to see the place my daughter died."

"Of course," Juniper replied, leading the way up the first flight of stairs. "Why don't you tell me about your problem, while we walk?"

Helen paused at the top of the stairs, putting her hand on the second-floor balustrade. "I think I'm being stalked by Kaitlyn's killer."

"You think?"

"Yes. No. I mean, I'm sure I'm being stalked."

Helen's responses grew more hesitant, and Juniper knew she was reconsidering being here at all. Juniper's heart went out to the woman. Her confusion and fear seemed genuine and so out of character from everything Juniper had seen of this strong tornado of a woman.

"Do you have any idea who's stalking you?" Juniper asked, yanking the door to the attic open.

Helen nodded as Juniper looked back.

Okay, Juniper thought. She's afraid to trust you. "Can you tell me?" She asked again pacing up the small and narrow attic stairwell.

"N-not exactly."

Juniper's back tightened and her pulse ticked up a notch. "Helen, if you know who killed your daughter then we need to go to the police. I'll go with you. Actually, I'll call them for you right now."

"No… no." Helen took a deep breath and blew it out. "You see, I can't... I don't know for sure yet. I'm trying to get evidence and, well, let's just say it's not just me who will be hurt if I'm wrong."

Juniper blinked. Surely, she'd heard incorrectly. "I'm sorry. I don't understand. What could be more important than bringing your daughter's killer to justice—especially if her killer's now stalking you? Does this have something to do with you slapping Peter yesterday outside your house?"

Helen paused, and Juniper wondered if she'd pushed too hard.

"It's a long, twisted story."

"I'm listening."

"I-I don't even know where to start."

"Maybe you should start at the beginning."

Helen nodded and then wandered to one of the dormer windows peering out in obvious paranoia. Dust motes careened around in the shafts of light. "Okay, but this is between us… I met Peter twenty-five years ago in Las Vegas before Lulu or anyone else knew him. I had just finished school, and I was pregnant with Meaghen. My parents all but told me I was marrying Frank Patone, so I packed up my car and headed to Vegas. I had a fling with Peter. He was charming and handsome, and we had fun together. I finally came to my senses a week later, and I returned to Bohemian Lake to marry Frank. Two years later, Peter showed up. He'd somehow found out where I lived."

"You hadn't told him?"

"No. Are you crazy? I knew my parents would never let me be with him."

Juniper sipped her coffee as Helen talked, trying to fathom marrying someone her parents had dictated.

"Anyway, for a while it was good," Helen said. "Frank worked a lot and so I saw Peter on the side."

"You were having an affair?"

"Please don't judge me. Peter and I loved each other, but I knew it was wrong. We were bound to get caught. Frank wanted to go into politics, and our life would be an open book. Plus, Frank wanted more children, although he was never home to get me pregnant, and he barely paid attention to little Meg. We never fought. Never even argued, but there wasn't any love." She paused for several seconds and appeared to be gathering her thoughts. Then she leaned against the wall and cried.

Juniper stood there for the first few seconds, unsure what to do with herself. Eventually, she put her arm around her shoulders, still wary since how well did she really know the woman. Helen leaned into her and cried even harder.

She didn't hold anything back and by the time she was done, her eyes were red and swollen, her nose was dripping everywhere and Juniper's shoulder was soaked in tears and snot.

When she was nearly dehydrated, she reached into her purse and pulled out a small package of tissues. She put one to her nose and blew with the force and noise of a large goose. She wadded up the tissue and tucked it in her pocket. "I'm so sorry," she said, grabbing another tissue and dabbing at her eyes and mottled cheeks. "I didn't mean to lose it like that."

"It's okay. I know this must be hard."

"Anyway, I broke it off with Peter and he left me alone for a while, but he refused to move. Eventually, he met my cousin Lulu, he was different at first. I thought maybe he really loved her. But then he found out I was pregnant with Kaitlyn and he started showing up at my house after Frank left for work. He was convinced that Kaitlyn was his child."

"Was she?"

Helen gave Juniper a sad smile. "I suppose she could have been. I don't think so, but I don't really know and I never wanted to."

"That's a lot to live with," Juniper said.

"As Kaitlyn got older," Helen continued, "I noticed Peter took an unhealthy interest in her. Kaitlyn was very close to her Aunt Lulu so I couldn't very well stop her from going over there. Finally, when she turned thirteen, I had enough, and I told him to stay away from her.

"Then he got mean. It was subtle at first—insults that he claimed were jokes—but it progressed and it undermined my relationship with my daughter.

"Kaitlyn thought I was jealous of Lulu but I was just more fearful that Peter had turned his obsession with me onto her."

"I'm sorry. That must have been a hard situation to navigate."

"Thank you. It was, especially since I never knew when and if Peter was going to blow the lid off the whole thing. Anyway, I finally spoke with Peter before Kaitlyn was murdered. I told him that I was going to tell everyone the truth and we could once and for all find out who her father was."

"What did Peter say?"

"He was furious. I think in some warped way he had fallen in love with Kaitlyn and he no longer saw himself as a possible father figure. It disgusts me to think about it but they may have even been having an affair."

"So why would he kill her?" Juniper allowed her eyes to peruse the servants' quarters before they headed back down the stairs. She tried to think of what could have happened the night Kaitlyn was there. According to what the detective had been willing to share, the authorities were assuming Kaitlyn had been having a romantic rendezvous that turned heated, but if Helen was already threatening to expose him then what risk would Kaitlyn pose? Unless she was trying to break it off with him?

"I don't know but he's definitely not stable." She took a deep breath and blew it out. "There is only one other option but I just can't even contemplate it."

"What? That it wasn't Peter at all—you think maybe Frank found out about the affair and killed Kaitlyn because she wasn't his kid?"

"No. No. Frank couldn't care less about any of us. As long as it doesn't mess up his career." She crossed her arms and shivered. "No, I'm worried Lulu found out."

"Lulu? But she's so sweet."

"Yes, sweet and naïve and also emotionally unstable—she's had her problems. Peter's had her committed a few times. Anyway, lately she's been awful snappy—you saw how she was the other day."

Helen stopped talking and her jaw flexed.

"You're worried that she'll go to jail?" Juniper asked.

Helen stared at the wall behind Juniper. "It would be my fault. I did this to her and her rotting in jail or an institution wouldn't bring Kaitlyn back." Helen swallowed hard. "But then I think to myself what if that monster did it—he deserves to go to jail—except again it's Lulu who would suffer the most. She loves him so much."

Juniper frowned. Love was so messed up—thank god she didn't have to deal with it. "I can't imagine…" She started her reply but stopped when she realized she was being disingenuous. "So why did you want to come here? How can I help you, Helen?"

"I just thought maybe if I looked around where Kaitlyn was killed, I could find a clue that would tell me whether it was Peter or Lulu who did it," Helen said. "But I was wrong." She looked directly at Juniper. "It was a mistake to come here. Please forget everything I told you." Helen wiped her eyes and nose and sniffed for a minute more. "I'm sorry," she said once she regained a semblance of control. "I thought I could handle this."

"Please don't apologize. I think you should go to the police."

Helen gave her a small smile. "Maybe. But, please don't say or do anything."

"As long as you're not in danger," Juniper's response was immediate, and more importantly, the truth. "I'll be there if you need someone to go with you."

Helen nodded. "Thank you. Deep down, I knew I could trust you."

Helen rose from the couch and pulled her purse over her shoulder. Juniper followed her to the front door. As Helen stepped outside, Juniper put a hand on her shoulder. "Helen, can I ask you a question?"

"Of course."

"Do you really want to go ahead with the Halloween Ball?"

Helen smiled. "The show must go on, my dear."

Juniper frowned. That was the saddest thing she'd heard her say.

"Anyway, I really do have to go. I have a lot to do before tonight."

"Tonight?"

"A charity board meeting. I have meetings twice a week."

Again, Juniper didn't want to judge, but how strange that this woman would go to board meetings when her daughter had just died. Oh well, everyone grieved differently—or so Eve had said. "Which charity? We occasionally donate on behalf of the business."

"You know I'm on a few different ones. Tonight is… Oh, I'm sorry my phone is vibrating and I know I have to take this call." Helen was already walking away as she spoke.

Juniper headed into the parlor where a box of props—skulls and fake bones — were waiting for her on the wine-colored brocade settee. She placed the skulls atop some old books on the mantle. It worked well with the gothic carving on the stone fireplace. She hated decorating but the show must go on, according to Helen, and she somehow doubted the decorating committee would be willing to come back to the house after Kaitlyn's death. Not that she blamed them.

TEN

J uniper stood on a ladder, edging the seams of the dining room. Their usual painters were all booked up this week, so it was up to her. Jack was hopeless when it came to detail work.

"Detective," Juniper said, glancing down at the fine-looking man walking into the foyer. "What are you doing back?"

"Can a police officer not randomly tour a crime scene?"

Juniper chuckled, hoping that he had intended that as a joke.

A half-smile played around his lips as he looked at her. "I had a few questions for you. I see you're busy. You are very hands on. It's not often you see a woman willing to get so dirty."

"My, my, aren't you quite the sexist?" Juniper said with a laugh. "I like painting and it's better than twiddling my thumbs."

"I'm sorry. I didn't mean to offend you. It's probably too early for me to do that yet. I just meant that you're a rare find and your boyfriend is very lucky to have you."

Juniper climbed down the ladder stairs and looked at him curiously. "I don't have a boyfriend. Jack is my business partner, remember, and he's engaged."

He offered up a toothy grin. "That's right. To your frenemy from the party. I just assumed there was someone else in the picture," he said, reaching out and touching her forehead.

"What are you doing?"

"Paint," he said with a laugh, "Sorry. I didn't mean to cross any lines there. You have paint on your face."

Juniper swiped her forehead with a towel and smiled. "Hazard of the job. So… you wanted to ask me something?"

"I did. I heard you spent the night here—the night of the murder. I don't mean to sound accusatory but Helen can be rather difficult at times and I'm ruling out people with alibis. Were you with someone?"

"No."

"You must be the bravest lady I know," he said with a grin. "Not afraid the ghost will get you?"

"Don't start," Juniper said with a smirk.

He laughed. "Can't help myself."

"Pike and I worked till almost seven then I went to her place for dinner. We made pasta and had some wine and she walked me back home around 9:30p.m. I attempted to finish up the tiling but a combination of the red wine and the hard work hit me and I went to bed after Pike left."

He jotted down some notes. "Good to know. You didn't see anyone hanging around?"

"Nope."

"What about any unusual vehicles as you were leaving?"

"Just the red sports car earlier that morning. Actually, I guess I may have heard car doors and voices when I was locking up but nothing out of the ordinary. People come and go all the time on the street. It's a main street."

"And your business partner, did he have dinner with the two of you?"

"No, Jack was still here when we left but I don't think he stayed long. His girlfriend is rather," she paused, searching for the right word, "high maintenance and she was waiting on him at home."

"Understood. The place looks beautiful by the way. You guys are doing a great job renovating it. I can see you are a force to be reckoned with. I hope that ghost realizes it's going to have to find a new place to live." He glanced toward the door. "Well, I guess there's not much more I can do tonight. Please call me if you think of anything else. I'm pretty handy with a hammer." He reached into his pocket and brought out a business card and a pen. He flipped it over in his hand and wrote down a number. "This is my home number. If anything happens, call me, okay? I don't want to find you in a trunk next."

"If someone tries to kill me, you'll be the first to know."

"Any time of night, Juniper, it doesn't matter," he said persistently. "If you need me, just call and I'll rush right over, even if you just want company for dinner."

Juniper smiled, thinking she just might give him a call.

"Can I make a suggestion?"

Normally, Juniper would never break a friend's trust, but Detective Lumos wasn't just anyone, and given what Helen had told her, he needed to be pointed in the right direction.

"I think you should take a closer look at Peter."

"Because of the red sports car?"

"Yes, but also because of other things. Look, Detective Lumos—"

"Call me Cody."

"Okay, Cody, I can't tell you everything because I promised a friend that I wouldn't and it's not my place, but I can tell you that Peter freaked out at Kaitlyn's funeral. I then saw him arguing with Kaitlyn's mother Helen in the backyard. Helen Patone is a nice woman, and she looked scared to death of him."

The Detective nodded. "In my job, I'm not allowed to speculate but let's just say I'm already headed down that road so you needn't worry."

Juniper set her paint brush down and rubbed her temples. "Good, but maybe if you could watch him a little more carefully just to make sure he's not following anyone, if you catch my drift."

Lumos nodded. "You think Peter is harassing the Patones? Why haven't they come forward?"

Juniper changed up her stance. "Let's just say there could be more to the story there. Families are never perfect but they do tend to stick together."

Lumos tapped one finger on the wall. Luckily, she hadn't painted over there yet. "Can you tell me anything that's not vague and confusing?"

Juniper sighed and shook her head just as Jack came in the door with their realtor—his father, Jack Sr., and Juniper realized all three men were staring at her. She suddenly felt horribly self-conscious. Her dust-and-grime-encrusted coveralls hung on her like a baggy, dirty jumpsuit and she didn't even want to think about what her hair looked like.

"Hey there, daughter-in-law, what are you doing covered in dirt. Is my son making you do all the work again?" Jack Sr. smiled as he marched in through the front door and swept Juniper up into a big bear hug.

"Daughter-in-law?" Cody asked.

Juniper blushed.

"He just calls her that. An old nickname," Jack clarified.

"Detective Lumos, this is Jack Sr. He's Jack's dad and the best realtor in the world."

"Actually, we've met. He sold me my house and I agree he is the best."

"Nice to see you again, Cody. How are you enjoying our fine little town?" Jack Sr. shook Cody's hand with the verve normally reserved for a professional wrestling match. To his credit, Cody appeared to give as well as he got. "You've met Juniper, here? Lucky man! She is a treat!"

"That she is," Cody said.

Jack Sr., guffawed, clapped him on the back, and then nodded at his son.

"Come on, Cody, I'll take you up to the attic so you can have a look around. I assume that's why you're here," Jack said.

No sooner were the two men headed up the stairs then Jack Sr., turned on Juniper. He stood back and looked her over. "So, what's new, beautiful? Have you stolen Jack away yet?"

Juniper shook her head playfully. "Jack is engaged to someone else, remember," Juniper said.

"This is true," Jack Sr. said, puffing out his chest. "But he will only ever love you."

"Yeah, yeah, what are you doing here?"

"I want to take some pictures. I have lots of potential buyers for this place."

"But it's not even done yet."

"No problem. We'll update the pictures later. How can I tease people without them?"

Jack picked up the camera that hung around his neck and began shooting the parlor first with its fireplace and old stained-glass window. There were several paintings in gold-gilt mirrors, and a lovely antique crystal chandelier that decorated the space.

After Jack Sr., left, Juniper stared out the laundry room window as she cleaned her paint brushes. Every so often, she'd catch sight of Jack in the distance. It was well after six, and he was packing up his tools for the day. A voice in her head told her to go talk to him. Ask him to stay the night so she wouldn't have to be alone here, but that wouldn't be fair. Besides, she wasn't some helpless princess who needed protecting, she argued back. That was the other woman in his life.

He was probably already gone, anyway. She reached into her purse and pulled out her phone. Seven missed calls from Pike. She shoved the phone back in her purse and zipped it up. What did she want so badly? She'd head over there for dinner and see.

She looked around, realizing all the volunteers were gone, and shrugged the straps down on her painter's overalls.

The paint-splattered pants hit the floor before she could pull her tights from her bag. She was standing in nothing but a white crop top and black lace underwear when Jack strolled into the front entranceway.

"Did you see all that excitement across the road?" he asked.

She grabbed her pants and shoved one leg inside them, stifling a small surprised yelp. Tripping forward she tried to get the other leg on. He reached out and gripped her elbows to steady her. "Wow, Juniper, have you been working out? You've got some abs popping there."

Smiling shyly, she took a step back.

His smile fell and a worried look crossed his face. "Sorry about that. I just came in to check on you."

He drummed his fingers on the wall and stepped into the dining room to change the subject, "The blue looks good, huh?"

She nodded, still feeling slightly embarrassed. Why couldn't she have been wearing a matching set of bra and underwear today? She slipped her brown cardigan on and followed him into the room. "I forgot how much work it was to paint a room with high ceilings and original trim."

"I bet. So, listen, I know I'm not your… well… you know… I lost the right… what I mean is… I don't think you should be alone tonight… here at the house."

"Why not?" She asked, her heart beating fast. "I always stay on the reno site. There isn't exactly a nice motel around here."

"I'd just feel better if I knew you were safe at Pike's."

"Protecting our investment is part of the job. Since when are you worried about me getting hurt? Besides, you used to stay all the time, too. How come you stopped staying over?"

He looked over at her and slowly smiled. He looked the very picture of the Cheshire Cat with his mischievous green eyes and bright white teeth set in an unnaturally wide smile. "Hmm, I wonder why."

She realized they were having another one of those conversations again. The kind that set her teeth on edge. Were they flirting or was it just her imagination? She almost wished he would start being a jerk so that she could stop wondering if he was toying with her.

"Well, what do you suggest, Jack? Want me to come sleep at your place instead?" She teased.

"Actually, I would love that… I mean you could if you need a place." He stumbled.

She looked back at him in irritation. "I'm sure Big Boobs… I mean Sally would love that." She suspected that he really did care about her, but she just didn't need the confusion at this point in her life. "Don't worry about me. Detective Lumos asked me to have dinner so I might not be alone."

Jack's eyes narrowed. "Why are you going out with him?"

"You were the one who said you didn't want me to be alone."

"Well I didn't mean you needed to sell yourself to the local cop for protection."

She snatched up her purse and headed for the door. "Shouldn't you be getting home to the warden?"

Jack raised his eyebrows.

"There's no need to get personal," he said in an unpleasant tone.

"Personal," Juniper said impatiently. "I believe you started this."

Jack's scowl disappeared and his face went blank. "You're right. I have no right to be jealous. Let's go. I'll walk you to your car."

"Don't bother. I'm walking," she said, strolling out the door. *Had he said jealous?* A smile played at her lips.

Halfway down the lawn, the skin on the back of her neck started to prickle. She stopped short and spun around, scanning the attic windows. No one was there. Nothing looked out of place.

But she could feel eyes on her.

She turned around and continued across the street, chiding herself for being jumpy like Helen.

ELEVEN

ookies & Corsets was officially closed when Juniper arrived; the cheerful yellow and black painted sign in the window invited her to check back tomorrow. She checked her phone. It was only 6:30. Why were they closed half an hour early? She peeked in the window. Lulu was slumped on the couch, surrounded by balled up used tissues. Pike smiled when she saw Juniper knock and hurried to open the door.

"Sorry about that—people kept coming in to ask about the police visit, nosey parkers."

"What happened?"

"The police came by looking for Peter, apparently he's under arrest but they can't locate him."

Lulu looked up at Juniper. Her bright green eyes were swollen and red with tears; her usual sleek black hair was wild and messy. "I'm so sorry, Lulu," Juniper said. She turned back to Pike. "Detective Lumos questioned me again as well, but he never mentioned anything about Peter."

"He didn't ask you what you overheard yesterday between Helen and Peter?"

"No. Why?"

"The police found a suitcase they say belonged to Kaitlyn in Peter's trunk—and they're suggesting that Peter and Kaitlyn were having an affair."

Lulu started to cry, and then Pike was rubbing her back and offering her tea. "Lulu suspected Peter was cheating, but she never suspected Kaitlyn."

"We're family," Lulu clarified. "Helen is my best-friend, and I always thought of Kaitlyn as a daughter. I feel so disgusted even thinking that any of this is true. They say Peter has run off."

My heart went out to her. What a pig Peter turned out to be. I couldn't help but think he'd tried to trade Lulu in for a younger model. After all, Kaitlyn was the spitting image of her aunt. Long dark hair, bright green eyes, and a tall and curvy frame, although, Kaitlyn hid her looks under dowdy clothes and thick glasses. Lulu had a few more wrinkles and her mid-section was a little fuller but she still very attractive.

"I called the bank and our account is empty. He withdrew all the money yesterday in cash."

Juniper bit her lip. Peter was looking more and more guilty.

"I don't mean to sound like a monster." Lulu hastened to say as she blew her nose once again. "I couldn't care less that that cheating bastard has run off, but he took all of our money. How am I going to support myself?"

"Did he sell the building to Frank after all?" Juniper asked.

Lulu looked up, shocked to see that Juniper knew about that.

"Pike told me she might need a new storefront."

Lulu nodded. "No. I don't think so."

"Well then you still have your business and your house."

"I guess."

The idea seemed to cheer her up and Juniper took the opportunity to suggest that they drive her home for food and rest.

TWELVE

L ulu lived on one of Bohemian Lake's charming tree-lined streets in an American Craftsman Bungalow with a low-pitched roof and a front porch not far from the old lumber mill. Though the house itself looked gorgeous from the outside with its Jack-o'-lanterns, hay bales and dried corn stocks, the foyer was a mess. A shattered vase lay on its side and several oil paintings were slashed to bits.

"What happened here?"

Lulu reached out and placed one hand on Pike's arm. She seemed to be muttering something unintelligible.

"Looks like Peter did some damage before he left," Pike said with obvious reluctance.

Inside, the rest of the place was worse. Dirty dishes covered the counters and little insects buzzed. The air smelled of stale cigarette smoke.

"My god, he's ruined the place." Lulu shook her head as she spoke. "I haven't been here in days. I've been sleeping at Helen's house because we were fighting."

"It's okay. We'll get the place all cleaned up, as good as new."

Lulu poured herself a glass of wine and sat down on a ripped armchair while Pike and Juniper tidied.

Juniper walked to the fireplace and picked up a photograph that lay at her feet. Sepia-toned and crumbling with age, it was of a family of six gathered on stiff looking chairs. Two men and two women and two young girls looking pretty in their frilly white finery, each girl rested her hand on her parent's shoulder. It was hard to tell, but the dress on the dark-haired woman looked familiar. Lulu grabbed the frame from her hand nicking her with the glass.

"That's mine," she shouted. "How dare he break it!"

Oww. Juniper stuck her thumb in her mouth. Shocked by Lulu's reaction.

Lulu was somehow already in a drunken state, after only had one drink. It seemed strange. A lightweight, Juniper supposed. She cradled the photo in her arms like a child.

"Peter must have smashed it." She began to cry again. "We had a fight on the weekend about him screwing around on me. He admitted that he had a secret but he wouldn't tell me about it. Can you believe that? Helen must have known about him and Kaitlyn. She was the one who first put me onto the idea. She said I shouldn't put up with that sort of thing. Peter was my first love. What am I going to do now? No man will want me."

"Lulu, listen to me," Pike said, putting one hand on her arm. "You don't need to attach yourself to some jerk. You are a strong, independent woman, in control of your own fate. Do you understand what I'm saying?"

Lulu shrugged and swallowed back another mouthful. She was on the cusp of passing out now and Juniper felt like an interloper. She picked up some of the discarded empty bottles and headed in search of a recycling bin.

When she opened the garage door, she was shocked to see Peter's prize cherry red Camaro. Why would a man who'd emptied their bank accounts willingly leave behind his prize possession.

THIRTEEN

In the distance, the low rattle of thunder let Jack and Juniper know the storm was inching its way toward them. Fallen leaves danced in the wind around their feet.

"I see a few of the volunteers were brave enough to come back to help." Jack said.

"Mayor Patone called in a few favors. With all that's happened, things are pretty behind schedule."

"And you really hate party decorating." Jack smiled as he stated this very true fact.

"And there's that," Juniper agreed. "I can handle the design and the overall concept but streamers and balloons are my kryptonite."

"I'm not sure a Halloween Ball calls for streamers and balloons, Junie. It's more like black lights and fake webs."

Juniper smirked. "See why I need help?" she turned and yelled, "Could we get these pumpkins carved? They need to line the walk." In addition to Axl there was Eve, Oliver, Pearl and Kingston. Only Kaitlyn was missing from this decorating committee but they all seemed in fine spirits, even somewhat excited for the party.

They each took a pumpkin and began to carve. "So, I heard a rumor that one of the girls in the neighborhood saw a ghost around here. Have you heard this?" Juniper asked. She was positive she was about to get laughed at but she wanted to get them talking.

The group nodded their heads as if she'd just asked the most common question in the world.

"Sure. Lots of neighborhood kids have seen the woman in white. She appears in the window sometimes," Axl said. "Why do you think the ghost tour is so popular and why do you think the town is so eager to check the place out on Halloween?"

Oliver grinned and held up his carving knife like a crazed lunatic. "They want to see if the legend is true. Will the Doctor and his wife come alive on Halloween?" Juniper quirked an eyebrow at the boy. She'd heard this mentioned on the tour. He went on. "They say the murder plays out, just like it did on that fateful Halloween."

"You guys," Kingston interrupted. "Can we not go there, please."

"Muhaha! They're coming to get you," Oliver said in an eerie voice, jumping up to tickle her from behind.

"Stop it," Kingston said. "Creeper."

Axl kept his head down and looked solemn. Perhaps this wasn't the best time for such grim topics but Juniper was really curious about the family's history. She bit her lip but couldn't hold her tongue. "I know the Doctor wasn't from here and he inherited a fortune and built this house as a wedding present for his bride… but what about Victoria? Was her family from Bohemian Lake?"

"Her family owned the saw mill in town," Oliver answered. "Her sister Marjorie and her husband, Almer lived next door." He pointed at Fern's place. "Almer's the one who heard the Doctor kill himself."

"How did he?" Juniper paused, carving out one of the ghoul's teeth. "You know, how did the doctor do it?"

"Gun to the head," Kingston replied sensibly. "After that, Marjorie and Almer tried to sell the place but no one would buy it. Then a huge fire hit the town, and they lost the saw mill. Almer decided he couldn't take it anymore. He was found right there, in the foyer, swinging from that big chandelier."

Juniper shivered. Hearing this story again was giving her the creeps. On the other hand… aside from Kaitlyn's murder in the attic, and the ghostly wanderer in the gardens, Juniper hadn't encountered any paranormal activity. No tormented murderer trying to make contact, for which Juniper was grateful.

"Have you seen the portrait?" asked Pearl.

"What portrait?"

"There was one in the attic. It hung on the east wall of the servant's quarters. It went missing around the same time Kaitlyn died. I assumed that you packed it up so it wouldn't get broken during the party."

"What did it look like?"

"It was a pewter-framed photograph in sepia tones. The Doctor and Victoria sat on stiff-looking chairs in the center of the portrait. To the left and slightly behind Victoria stood a woman about their age who looked a lot like her— her sister Marjorie. Next to her was an older man, probably Almer. And with them were two teenage girls."

"I could have sworn I saw a photo like that at Lulu's just the other night."

"Well, it would make sense for her to have one too. After all, the teenage girl in the photo was her Great-Great-Great-Grandmother," Pearl said.

"Right," Juniper agreed. Although she privately pondered the thought that maybe it was the exact portrait. Lulu had acted strange when she saw it. Had she stolen it from the house?

Juniper turned her head to the sound of a vehicle pulling up to the curb.

"Anyone commit a crime?" Kingston asked.

"Oh no, say what?" Mrs. Banter scrambled for her purse. "Hide the green stuff."

Kingston laughed. "I'm just kidding. It's just Juniper's hunky cop boyfriend."

"What? I don't have a boyfriend." Juniper turned and watched Detective Cody Lumos stepping from his car.

"Just the lady I was hoping to find," he said, as he reached them.

"Cody. Is everything okay?"

"Of course. I was just wondering if you'd like to get dinner and a drink?"

Juniper glanced at the smirk on the kid's faces. *Great, now they would tease her even more.* Pike wasn't expecting her for dinner, but still she felt weird saying yes.

"Come on, take pity on me. I can only make my own pasta and hot dogs for so long."

"What's Penny up to?" Eve asked.

Juniper looked at Cody and raised an eyebrow. She'd heard rumors that he'd been seeing one of the locals, an ex-cop turned private investigator, but she'd yet to see them together.

"How would I know? She's always busy and why are you asking me. You're the one who sees her every day."

Eve smirked and went back to carving. That woman loved to stir the pot.

"I'll go." Kingston piped up.

"Oh no, you won't." Mrs. Banter exclaimed.

"And why not? Juniper apparently doesn't want to go. I can't let this poor, fine man eat alone."

"You're underage, young lady."

"Underage. Since when does breaking the law matter to you? Give me your purse, I'll show Detective Lumos just what you think of the rules."

"Just never you mind, girlie." Mrs. Banter smirked. "And you better learn to shut that trap of yours or I'll add you to the rat list.

Cody turned back to Juniper and bit his lip. He was barely containing his laughter. "Juniper?"

"I'm sorry. I can't today. We're really behind schedule, but I'm free for lunch tomorrow if you are."

"Tomorrow is my day off so that will work out perfectly."

FOURTEEN

J ack and Juniper did a quick walk-through of the house to make sure they were on schedule with their preliminary scope of work. Spirited Construction did restorations right: completing every step of the process from A to Z. They stood outside on the sidewalk, looking up at the roofline as Juniper explained about the widow's walk and how some woman from the historic society had called and been adamant that they do not change any of the lines.

"Did you explain to them that we don't buy these historic homes to make them modern?" Jack said.

"Of course, I did."

"You can't blame her for making sure."

"I guess not. You would think they would have just looked at our track record. When have we ever—"

Juniper's words were cut off by the arrival of a woman. She was clutching a coffee cup and huddling in a wool sweater.

"Hey, there. Are you one of Pike's volunteers? No one told me—" Juniper said.

The woman shrugged. "No. I just wanted to introduce myself. I'm your next-door neighbor, Fern Baron. Although I'd love to lend a helping hand sometime."

"Hi, Fern." Jack stuck out his hand and Fern accepted it. "It's nice to meet you. Regrettably, I'm late to meet the plumber at another job but I look forward to seeing you again."

Fern smiled and both Juniper and Fern watched Jack jog to his truck. Then he turned back to Juniper. "Oh, hey, I picked up the original blueprints from Jared Mitchell. The old owners had them. They're on the dining room table. I'll see you tomorrow."

Juniper smiled and opened the massive wood door, holding the screen open for Fern. "Well, come on in, Fern. I'd offer to make you a coffee but I see you've already got one."

She smiled as she followed her inside. "I do. I can't stay long but maybe I can help out next week. I work at the hardware store in town."

"I'm sure we'll get to know one another well. My second home is the hardware store. As a matter of fact, I'm surprised we haven't met by now."

Fern laughed. "I could see that being true. I'm just coming off holidays."

She paused as if she wanted to ask her something but then said nothing. Juniper waited a moment but there was still just awkward silence.

"I should get to work. I'm hoping the ghosts are awake and out of the house."

"Have you seen them?" Fern asked as nonchalantly as if she were asking about the weather.

"Not really," Juniper answered, intrigued. This was clearly what Fern had been waiting to talk about. She didn't really seem like the type to gossip, so, what was this about? "You?"

"My daughter has. She sees the doctor's wife sometimes in the window, other times, on the hill behind the house. She even claimed to see the ghostly woman coming out of our carriage house once."

"Do you believe her?"

"She's always had quite the imagination, so it's hard to know if she's telling the truth. Although, sometimes I hear music."

Juniper nodded. "Anything else?"

Fern hesitated.

"Anything at all, no matter how bizarre or silly it sounds?"

"I once thought I heard a woman's voice, calling out. Sort of like a moan, but more than that? For all I know it's the teenagers, but it was… eerie."

"Can you describe the moaning?"

She shrugged. "Just sort of… a ghostly moaning. Or what I assume a ghost sounds like based on old horror flicks."

"So, you've heard music and a woman moaning."

She nodded. "But like I said, the moaning was just once and it might have been one of the neighbor's cats or a kid on the street, something not in the least bit supernatural. And I just sort of assumed the music was from a car passing by with a loud stereo system…"

"Blasting a waltz?"

Fern shrugged. "Now that you mention it, I guess that seems kind of unlikely."

"Any flickering lights or objects being moved around?"

"I'm not usually inside but there is a photo that I heard was moved around the house."

"What kind of photo?"

"Very old, sepia. It was the Doctor and Victoria and her sister's family." She paused. "Oh, I almost forgot, my absent-minded daughter left the carriage house door open and a stray cat got in. It took me twenty minutes just to get it out. Do you own a black cat with white paws?"

"Sorry, I don't."

"Well there's one on the loose." She smiled and glanced at her phone. "Anyway, I'm late now. Let's chat later."

Juniper waited for Fern to leave before heading into the dining room. The woman seemed nice but peculiar.

The dining room had dried nicely. She was happy with the shade of blue she'd chosen, now to move on to the next job. She did some quick scouting through the upstairs second floor where a massive fireplace occupied much of the master bedroom. She needed to check to make sure the fireplace worked. As she about to leave, something caught her eye.

The bedroom had a doorway into the next room but the wall seemed awfully thick. She checked the next bedroom, looking for a closet. Although they were rare in older homes, there had to be something that would account for the missing space.

Every house had hidden channels that held heating vents, air returns, pipes, and electrical wires. Old buildings often had large voids between the walls that had once been filled with stovepipes or chimneys that were no longer necessary. But a void in this location struck her as odd. There are reasons old houses were laid out a certain way, and this layout wasn't making sense.

She returned to the main floor and unrolled the heavy blueprints atop the dining room table.

Yep. There were areas left empty for no apparent reason. They did not contain electrical grids or vents, at least not according to the drawings. They were simply dead space. Worse, she realized as she examined the drawings closely, the blueprints didn't match the actual building in some places. For instance, the blueprints called for a twenty-five-foot-long bedroom, but the actual room wasn't a full twenty-five feet. She would bet her steel-toed boots on it.

Something's not right here. She unclipped a heavy tape measure from her belt and took a few quick measurements, then consulted the drawings. It wasn't her imagination: The blueprints did not match up with her measurements. Where was the missing square footage?

Her bag was in the attic. In it she had a tool that measured with a beam of light instead of a tape. She was headed up the attic steps when she heard music. It sounded as if it was coming from the landing, but when she got there, she realized the strains were coming from the dead space between the bedrooms. She put her ear up to the new wall.

Ta da tan, tan, tan… ta da tan, tan, toooon …

Whispers.

Juniper cast a compulsive glance over her shoulder and searched her peripheral vision, expecting to see a ghost.

She didn't see anything.

It was bright daylight, ghosts couldn't manifest, could they?

Giggles.

Then again ghosts probably didn't care much about the clock.

From behind the wall, the loud creak of the floor sounded.

Juniper pulled out her phone and searched for any references to Bohemian Lake Doctor's mansion.

The first thing to pop up was the real estate listing, with a professional photograph of the mansion. She clicked on a local history Web site that mentioned the Doctor's House had been built by Doctor Albert Downey in 1898. She scrolled through a few other sites, but there were no rumors of ghosts at the address.

"Whatcha doin?" Jack said, walking up the staircase.

"Jack. I thought you were meeting with the plumber?"

"Couldn't stay away, I guess."

Juniper raised an eyebrow.

"We rescheduled. What's so interesting on your phone? Your lips were moving… you only do that when you're super invested."

"You'd think you'd be a better lip reader by now, then, huh, Mr. Nosey?"

Jack laughed and nodded.

"I was just trying to find some more background info on the phone but I'm not seeing anything. I'm thinking maybe a trip to the Historical Society is in order."

"Why, are you making contact with spirits again?"

"Maybe. Do you ever hear music playing from behind the walls?"

"What kind of music?"

"A waltz."

"Can't say that I have but then again I always have my power tools on blast, at least the Doctor's House has classy ghosts."

"Mmm."

"By the way, I've been meaning to talk to about you something. Can we go sit downstairs and talk?"

Juniper set her phone down and turned her attention to Jack. "That sounds serious. Everything okay? Did we miss a payment on something?"

"Everything is fine. It's about..."

"About the business?" Juniper finished his sentence for him.

"It's just..." Jack swallowed. "Did you hear the door?"

"Hello? Anyone here?" A strange voice called out from below.

"That sounds like the detective. He was meeting me for lunch," Juniper explained. "I'll be right down," Juniper shouted before turning back to Jack. "What were you going to say?"

"It's nothing. Go on your date."

Juniper froze. "Jack? What is it? What's going on?"

"Nothing, I just have to go out of town for Halloween, so I won't be here for the ball. I didn't know how you'd feel about hosting the ball alone considering what's happened."

"That's it? Wow, that's just… wow. You trying to give me a heart attack? Pike will be here and besides I'm not really hosting. We're just lending them the house."

"Right, sorry. I didn't mean to make it sound that important," Jack reached out and touched her hand. "I just thought you might not like having to play chaperone on your own."

"Oh… yeah. I guess, but I won't be alone."

"No, I guess you won't be."

FIFTEEN

The pub in the next town over was full of dark wood paneling and oil paintings. It was the sort of place Juniper enjoyed and she was glad the detective had suggested it. Pretentious dudes were not her style.

"This place reminded me of the Doctors House so I thought you might like it," Cody said as they sat at a small table in the corner.

Juniper nodded, "Yes, it was a good pick, Detective, almost as if you were trying to put me at ease."

He smiled and winked. The waitress came and took their orders: a glass of wine for her, beer on tap for him. She was young and pretty, and clearly intrigued by Cody, who was paying no attention to her.

"So, I learned something interesting from one of the volunteers yesterday," Juniper said finally. "Apparently, there's a picture missing from the attic. An old family photo of the Doctor and his wife."

"Okay." He gave a humorless chuckle. "Is that somehow relevant to us?"

"Well, to be fair, it wouldn't seem so, however, I just happened to see a photo like that at Lulu's."

Cody looked up from his glass. "I'm sorry. I probably should have made this clear. I was asking you here on a date, so that means no shop talk."

Juniper laughed. "Yes, sir."

He fixed her with a look. "Tell me about you and Jack? What's the full story there?"

"I already told you."

He remained still, but his eyebrows lifted. "It's just sometimes I get the vibe that things aren't exactly over between you." He took a deep draw on his beer and tilted his head. "Am I right?"

"I'm not going to get into the specifics but trust me when I say we're over. He's getting married… I'd say that's pretty over."

"But you're not happy for him."

"Jack has been my best friend for many years. I'm protective of him, that's all. When he lost his best-friend at twenty, I was there for him. When my first apartment flooded, it was Jack who took me in. We've always had each other's backs. Anyone he marries or I date will need to be tolerant and respect our relationship."

"And she doesn't?"

"No. Sally is threatened by me. That's why I don't want him to marry her."

The way she said it was so forceful that even she almost believed her words. *Hey! Fake it 'til you make it, right? She thought.* The waitress came back with two burgers and a plate of smoked meat poutine, which was basically a heaping pile of smoked Montreal meat and fries smothered in cheese curds and gravy.

Cody picked up his burger and bit into it.

"Please," he said, pushing the plate toward her. "Help yourself."

"Thank you."

Juniper took a couple fries and then turned the table on him.

"So, what's up with you, Mr. Twenty-one questions? What's your story? Why are you this town's most eligible bachelor?"

He laughed. "Hardly."

"You seem pretty popular to me." She nodded at the waitress who was still openly staring and flirting. "Is it true you're seeing Penelope Trubble from the Bohemian Private Eye because she knows martial arts so I'd rather not mess with her?"

Cody gave Juniper a crooked smile and laughed. "Truthfully, I did kiss Ms. Trubble in the summer after we closed a case and we had a meal once or twice. She's an ex-cop and we relate on a level that most civilians don't."

"So, what's the problem? Why are you asking other women out?"

"It seems Penelope isn't ready to date anyone just yet. She's getting over a breakup and from what I've heard around town, she's also dating an editor from the magazine she freelances for. I'm not interested in playing second fiddle which is why I'm asking you about Jack."

The waitress chose that moment to come by. She asked him if there was anything, anything at all, she could get for him.

He gestured to Juniper's empty wine glass. "Yes, a refill for the lady, please."

The waitress returned with the wine and slipped Cody an extra napkin.

"Oh, thank you," he said. She gave him a smile full of promise, then left.

"Anyway, I can't seem to find a suitable young woman who doesn't have a complicated relationship with her ex…" He trailed off as Juniper reached over and turned his new napkin over.

Sure enough, the waitress had written down her name and number.

Juniper handed it back to him. "Go on. You were saying, you're so hard pressed."

Cody's face flooded with color. "I didn't mean to encourage her. I apologize."

Juniper smiled.

"You didn't encourage her," Juniper said. "However, you do seem to undervalue your charm."

Cody laughed and Juniper couldn't help but smile in response.

He shook his head, still chuckling, and stared at her for a long moment. "You really don't pull any punches, do you, Juniper Palmer?"

"I really don't," Juniper said.

SIXTEEN

J uniper appeared in the kitchen doorway of Cookies & Corsets, startling Pike into almost dropping the butter, sugar, flour, eggs and large bowl she was trying to balance in her arms. "I guess I missed the big customer lunch rush today."

"It's almost 3pm. What have you been up to all day? I didn't hear you leave this morning. Did you even get a coffee?" She settled the ingredients on the large prep island in the middle of the kitchen.

Juniper nodded, peeking into the oven to see the yummy cupcakes Pike had on the go. "Jack brought me coffee and a bagel sandwich but I'm hungry now." Pike worked the butter and sugar together in a large stainless-steel bowl.

"I was going to see if you wanted to come over for dinner tonight," Pike said cracking an egg. She set the bowl under one of her new mixers, turned the machine on low then watched as the beaters did the job of blending the ingredients. "We can drink wine and catch up on our gossip." Pike left the mixer, moving over to a rack of cooled cupcakes. Picking up a long knife, she slid it across the top of the pan, expertly slicing off the cupcake tops in order to ice the middle. "By the way, I can make up the spare bedroom for you if you want to stay for a while. That couch probably wasn't very comfortable."

Pike set the cupcake tops on a rack. Moving over to the mixer she turned it off, hefted the bowl, poured the batter into the little cups of a fresh cupcake pan and slid it into the oven.

"Thanks, but I don't want to inconvenience you. What with all of the hot dates you got on the go."

Pike rolled her eyes, eliciting a laugh from Juniper.

"Well, perhaps my dating life can be put on hold. Axl is the only one who flirts with me and I think he's got a girlfriend now." Pike finished up the butter cream and the sugary vanilla scent made Juniper's stomach growl. Pike smirked and handed one of the finished frosting stuffed cupcakes to Juniper just as the bell over the front door announced the arrival of a customer.

"Can you help whoever's out there? I've got to get these in the oven."

Juniper pushed through the door and saw a woman of about seventy standing at the glass.

She smiled when she saw her. Her brown hair was curled and plastered with hairspray into a giant bouffant.

"Well, now, you must be our newest resident? I was just coming to see Pike about a coffee and a fritter. I didn't expect to see you manning the place. You taking over the street?" she teased.

"Apparently, I'm a jack of all trades," Juniper said, pouring her a coffee and grabbing the tongs to reach in for a fresh apple fritter. "I saw you at the funeral, didn't I? You were with Helen, right?"

"Yes, I do confess to being there but trust me when I say I was not with Helen." She folded her arms across her ample chest. "I was simply there supporting my nephew Frank and his babies."

Juniper blinked but didn't say anything.

"I'm Lorraine. Frank's aunt. Helen and I don't really see eye to eye," she blew on the surface of her coffee. "We are amicable, but that's about it." For a moment her eyes teared up and Juniper thought she was going to have yet another woman break down in front of her.

"Are you okay?"

"I am. I'm sorry. I'm just emotional lately."

"That's okay," Juniper said. "I'm sure it's hard losing Kaitlyn like that."

She nodded and wiped at her eyes. "Yes. It is. I miss her terribly."

Juniper nodded. "Would you like some water? I could use some."

"Sure."

"I spent last night with the kids—Meg and Axl, they're heartbroken," she said, waving a hand in the air. "I'm just overly emotional for them."

She took a long sip from her coffee and it seemed to steady her. She took a deep breath and leaned back on her stool. "You know, Jack says really nice things about you."

"You know Jack?"

"Since he was knee high to a grasshopper," she smirked. "I lived here my whole life up until about a year ago. Now I live in the next town over but I'm here often enough and I saw Jack just yesterday."

Juniper smiled at her. "Jack and I are very close or we used to be."

"He still loves you," she said. "I mean, I know he's with Sally, but anyone with eyes can see how he feels about you."

Juniper wondered if that were true.

Her face clouded over and she stared into her coffee again. "Relationships are funny, aren't they?"

Juniper nodded. "If I may ask, why don't you and Helen get along?"

Lorraine's eyes narrowed, and she set her cup down on the table. She placed her hands flat on her thighs and looked at Juniper.

"Because," she said, glowering. "She is a stupid, horrid, waste of a human life."

Now they were getting somewhere.

"I'm sorry, that was blunt, wasn't it?" Lorraine said, picking up her coffee mug again.

"But why's that?" Juniper asked, trying to sound vaguely interested without coming off as totally intrusive.

"Mainly because I think she's a lying shrew."

"Oh."

She stared at the mug like she was going to take a bite out of it. "That woman was bad news for my nephew from day one. But he wouldn't listen to me. I tried to warn him off, but he just got sucked in by that succubus." She snarled at the cup and took a sip. She licked at her lips. "I can't think of one good thing that has come from their relationship. Not one good thing."

Juniper looked around, thinking of the three kids she'd just mentioned, but decided not to comment. "So, you would be happy if they got a divorce?"

"Oh, you betcha," she said, nodding furiously. "Most definitely. I would be so glad. It wouldn't be soon enough if I never saw her again. She's a horrible creature who would be better off living at the bottom of a lake where she could bottom feed for the rest of her pathetic life," she said. "Among other things."

"Right," Juniper said, sipping her water.

She waved her hand in the air. "We just didn't get along. At all. Anything that interested Frank, Helen would belittle or dismiss. The only things that mattered were the things that mattered to Helen." Her eyes narrowed again. "And I think she stepped out on him with that brother-in-law of hers."

"You mean had an affair?"

She tugged at the lapel on her blazer. "Frankie told me I didn't know what I was talking about, but I always had a suspicion. No proof, so there wasn't anything I could do about it." A small smile creased her lips. "She always wanted what Lulu had. Poor Lulu. When Lulu told me her and Peter were getting married, I couldn't help but hug her. That sweet girl deserved happiness."

"I'm sure," Juniper said.

"Helen wasn't happy though," she said, still smiling. "Pretty sure there was a lot of crying after that ceremony." She shook her head. "She was not happy that day in any way at all."

The wheels were spinning in Juniper's head. "But I heard that it was Peter who wanted her."

She shook her head. Adamantly. "No way, no how." Lorraine smiled.

Juniper pressed her lips together and thought back to her conversation with Helen. That was a far different story than what she'd told at the house.

RACHAEL STAPLETON

SEVENTEEN

The next day Juniper lingered outside the property in her FJ Cruiser, sizing up the mansion's beautiful Victorian exterior while placing a few calls. First things first: she dialed a certain local psychic. She had a few more questions about Ms. Kaitlyn Patone and her mysterious lover. Pearl's soft voice burst into laughter when Juniper mentioned Peter and his red Camaro.

"You can't be serious. Who told you that? Was it Helen? You know she wasn't Kaitlyn's real mom, right? Bring me dinner at five—I like sushi."

"Excuse me? How do you know that?"

"I have back-to-back clients all day so if you want to see me then you'll bring me dinner at five."

"They don't have sushi here," Juniper clarified. "I just need five minutes to talk to you about Kaitlyn—and who she was seeing."

"I understand that but, believe me, it will take more than five minutes. Chinese is good, too—something with noodles. Got to go. My three o'clock is here."

She hung up before Juniper could respond. She texted Pike to let her know that dinner would be delivered to her doorstep—sesame chicken and shanghai noodles and since Juniper was paying for it, she decided she would get Pearl's take on her life—in particular, some guidance on what to do about Jack. He was the perfect partner if only he wasn't engaged to the devil's handmaiden and… if only she didn't still love him. Give Juniper water damage over a romantic relationship any day. Love was so much harder to repair.

She hit up the hardware store, then returned several calls from suppliers and checked in with Jack.

After that she picked up dinner and headed for Pine Street. It wasn't far, so she decided to walk. Pearl's house turned out to be in a split-level brick bungalow. The note on the front door said to use the back entrance.

The gate latch was a little tricky but once Juniper got it open, the path was clear. She turned right and spied the back door.

"Pearl?" She called. "It's Juniper. Juniper Palmer. I've got your dinner."

No answer.

The main door was open and the screen door wasn't latched. She could have sworn she heard sobbing coming from inside the house. She cautiously pulled the screen door open a crack and called her name again. There was a phone ringing from somewhere inside. Why wasn't she answering her phone, and that's when she saw her on the floor, in a pool of bright red blood.

EIGHTEEN

There was a young man in the room, down on one knee, leaning over the body. At Juniper's footsteps he turned and whispered, "Call nine-one-one."

Juniper instantly recognized the voice. Then her eyes lit upon what looked like a butcher knife lying on the floor next to Pearl. It was covered in blood. Her stomach lurched.

"Axl." He looked pale—probably suffering from shock. Juniper assumed he was re-living his sister's murder. Either that or he was the murderer, and he was overcome with regret. A cellphone on the table to her left began vibrating. The name, Hatti flashed on the screen. Juniper pulled out her own cell phone and punched in Detective Lumos's number. He answered on the second ring.

"Juniper. Just the woman I was thinking of. You ready to take me up on that dinner invite?"

"Not quite," she said, and gave him Pearl's address.

"What's the situation? Anybody else there?"

Juniper turned away from Axl, who remained beside the body. "Axl," she whispered.

"Wasn't he also there when you found his sister in the trunk?"

"He was here when I got here."

"Go outside. I'm five minutes away."

Juniper hung up. "Shouldn't be long now. He suggested we go outside and get a breath of fresh air."

Juniper felt awkward as Axl followed her out the back door. "What were you doing here? Did you have an appointment for a reading?"

"No. I just dropped in."

"You drop in on Pearl often?"

"We were dating," he replied.

"Oh, I… I'm so very sorry for your loss."

"Thank you." His eyes glistened with tears, but his voice showed little emotion. "Wait—why were you coming here? You weren't friends with Pearl. I mean, sorry, that was rude, I just meant you only just moved here and met her."

"I know. You're right. Pearl asked me to come. I called her today and asked her some questions about your sister. She didn't have time to talk."

"Kaitlyn?" Axl said with a squint, then looked toward the sound of distant sirens. "Why were you asking about Kaitlyn?"

They waited in silence for a few moments as the sirens drew closer.

"I wanted to talk to her about your sister's boy—" Juniper realized with a start that someone had killed Kaitlyn for what she knew and suddenly opening up didn't seem very smart.

His eyebrows rose, just a smidgen.

"Boyfriend?" he asked. "You were trying to find out if Kaitlyn had a boyfriend? Why?"

"I just saw her get picked up in this car and it occurred to me that—you know what—never mind. It was stupid, and this isn't the time."

The gate opened and two uniformed officers strode over to them. Juniper automatically raised her hands and stepped away from the door to allow them to enter.

"I was the one who called Detective Lumos," Juniper said, her hands still in the air.

"He's right behind us," one cop barked. "Stay here and wait for him."

"And you stay right here too," the other police officer said to Axl. Juniper could see through the door that the first cop in had placed two fingers on Pearl's neck, checking for signs of life. He shook his head and spoke softly into his radio.

Detective Lumos chose that moment to appear. He was tall, muscular, a dedicated professional with a no-nonsense air. There was never any question as to who was in charge when he was in the room. He nodded at Axl, then zeroed in on Juniper.

"Are you alright?" he said.

"I am," Juniper said, relieved.

"You know, it's downright eerie how often I find you at murder scenes," the Detective said.

"I had an appointment, and I swear when I arrived, she was already dead."

"I'm going to assume we'll find some sort of connection between your latest haunted house and this situation."

"Well, I think there's a connection—that's why I'm here. I wanted to ask Pearl about Kaitlyn. You know, find out who she was seeing. They were best friends after all."

"Her family said she didn't have a boyfriend."

"I know, but I started to wonder about Peter. You know he drives a red Camaro and Lulu thinks he's having an affair. So, I called Pearl, but she laughed at the idea. She suggested Helen put me up to that line of thinking. She was going to fill me in when I got here but of course I was too late."

They both took a moment.

"Okay," he said with a sigh. "That about it?" Juniper nodded. "You can go. I know where to find you for follow-up."

"And you?" Lumos said, turning back to Axl.

"Pearl and I were dating," he said. "I stopped in to bring her flowers because we'd had a fight yesterday."

"A fight…?"

"Nothing serious," he said quietly. "Her and my mother didn't exactly get along."

"I see," Cody said, conveying a lot in a few words. Helen wasn't the easiest person to get along with. "I'm sorry for your loss, Mr. Patone."

"Thank you."

"Did you find her exactly like this?"

He nodded.

"All right. Let me take a look at the scene, and then we'll have a little chat." He raised his chin in Juniper's direction. "You can go, I'll be in touch later."

"Yes sir," Juniper said.

Axl glanced at Juniper. "You two seem awfully friendly. You dating him now?"

Juniper started to say something snide about it being none of his business, but reconsidered. His sister and his girlfriend had just been murdered after all. Assuming he didn't do it, the least she could do was cut him a little slack.

"Sorry. I'm being rude again. I'll never forgive myself for not arriving an hour earlier. Or perhaps even fifteen minutes earlier… Whatever it would have taken to avoid this tragedy or my sisters."

Axl's voice caught in his throat, and his emotions seemed genuine. Unless he was a first-class actor, which, for all Juniper knew, he was.

Detective Lumos appeared in the doorway. "Follow me, please, Mr. Patone."

They disappeared into the bungalow. Juniper remained in the hall and watched the forensics team arrive, loaded down with bags of equipment. A few neighbors stuck their heads out of their houses to check on the hubbub. Juniper did her best to avoid their curious gazes.

The most pertinent question at the moment, for her at least, was if Pearl's death had anything to do with Kaitlyn's. Certainly, it seemed that way.

NINETEEN

Juniper stumbled inside the café ready to start another workday.

"Mornin'," Pike called out as she sipped coffee and read her tablet at the bakery counter. "Sleep well?"

"I did, actually," Juniper said, walking behind and pouring coffee from the pot into a commuter cup. "That nerve pill you gave me did the trick. Thank you."

Pike fixed Juniper with a look. "You're not going to find any more dead bodies, are you? Because I only have so many pills left."

Juniper smiled. "I'll try to keep that in mind."

"Good," Pike said, getting to her feet. "So, did your boyfriend say whether or not Axl Patone is a suspect?"

"My boyfriend?"

"Detective Cody."

"Oh, lord. Your life is a romance novel, isn't it?"

Pike smiled. "Can't say the same for you, my friend."

"No, you definitely can't. Anyway, as far as I know they don't have anything in particular to make them think so—other than me."

"You?"

"Yeah, well, I saw him kneeling over the body."

"Well, yeah—but you said he wasn't stabbing her, just kneeling there looking like he was about to cry. Is there something you're not telling me?"

"No. I just mean my statement is the only obvious reason they might have to suspect him but I think he's innocent and I'm sure the forensics will prove that."

"Cool."

"Why do you want to know?"

"Well, it's just he's always hitting on me and you never know when a girl might feel frisky. Now that he's single again."

"Oh my goodness, Pike, you are something else."

Pike smiled. "Why don't you sit down and I'll get you breakfast."

"It's okay. I made an egg before I left your place. I'll stop in later for more caffeine and sugar pick-me-up. I need to go to the Hardware store to grab some supplies that I forgot yesterday."

The doorbell jingled and Lulu came in the front door, carrying a bag. "Oh hey, Juniper, just the lady I was thinking of. I have the perfect dress for you."

"A dress?"

"A Halloween costume." She opened the bag and pulled out a pink striped gown. It was completely over the top, but beautiful.

"Where did you get that?"

"It's an antique—a silk and satin evening dress passed down through my family, but it suits you, it really does," Lulu said. "Just look at that underskirt with the pleating around it. The basque bodice with the low square neck and the vest… oh, it is one of my favorites. Want to try it on?"

"How could I refuse?"

"What do you have for me?" Pike chimed in.

"Are you done here? Follow me and we'll play dress-up."

Lulu led the way to her half of the store and plucked an armful of dresses from one of the racks and carted them in the direction of the dressing room.

Pike turned to Juniper and winked. "Perks to sharing a shop with her."

"Yes, and the perks to sharing a shop with you makes me chain myself to the treadmill… but I love it," Lulu retorted. "Now, let's see, Pike. Were you thinking of going as one of the elite, or perhaps a servant? I've had a whole shipment of dresses and accessories brought in to accommodate the Ball's costumes, or I can pull from my vintage section."

"Let's try them all, starting with the naughty chambermaid."

Lulu ran back and forth, bringing Pike sashes and bustiers while simultaneously entertaining Juniper.

Eventually, after fifteen minutes of feeling like a kid playing dress-up, Juniper had been layered and looked like an authentic Victorian lady. Pike looked more austere in a high collared black silk brocade tea gown. They stood back and admired themselves in the mirror: They looked like they had just stepped out of a different time.

"Show Juniper what you're planning to wear." Pike turned to gush, "it is absolutely ethereal. I want to steal it. There's a matching smaller version, but it's for a teenage girl and you know how tiny their waists were back then."

Lulu ran to the back and returned a minute later. "Presto," she said pulling it from the protective bag. "A cotton gauze and Valenciennes lace summer day dress. Isn't it darling?"

"It's beautiful. It looks like the white dress in that photo?" Juniper said.

"It is. All of these gowns were passed down to me. I just need to find my matching parasol. This is what I love about vintage," Lulu said softly.

Lulu twirled in front of the mirror, her eyes glazing over once again. "We will look so refined. Of course, the line between the worlds is thin on Samhain, and with it being the anniversary of the murder, hopefully the Doctor doesn't confuse one of us with the real Victoria."

"Yes, hopefully he's not into house calls," Juniper joked, but Lulu's face remained serious. Her eyes had that glazed look once again, and she was softly humming to herself. The song sounded familiar, but Juniper couldn't quite place it.

TWENTY

J ack spent the morning finishing up renovations at the mansion while Juniper and a few helpers moved in the mélange of furniture and décor Juniper used to stage the houses they flipped. By the time Jack finished the bathroom tile, June had staged the main floor. They took twenty enjoyable minutes to catch up over coffee. Not once did he mention the devil woman which she was thankful for.

Afterward, Juniper headed to the hardware shop to pick up some picture anchors for the upstairs paintings. The decorating crew was back at the mansion working steadily and didn't seem to require her help. And besides, she had other things on her mind.

Unfortunately, she wasn't the only one out and about in the small town of Bohemian Lake.

"Juniper!" Helen Patone gushed, as if they were long lost friends. "I'd like you to meet my husband, Frank."

"Ah, Juniper, nice to finally meet you," Frank said.

She'd actually met Frank twice since she'd been in town but clearly Juniper wasn't that memorable. She had noticed in her brief three weeks in town that the mayor talked at people instead of to them and avoided eye contact often. It made her wonder how he got elected unless no one else ever ran against him. Juniper gave a mental shrug. The mayor's politics were none of her concern.

"Nice to meet you as well," Juniper lied, as if she'd never heard of the man.

"And this is our daughter, Meg."

"How do you do?" Juniper said and nodded politely in return.

"Juniper is the one who bought and is renovating the Doctor's House."

Juniper nodded. "Yes, I was just on my way to the hardware store to pick up some last-minute supplies."

"That's handy!" said Frank. "We were just on our way to lunch."

"Sure you don't want to join us?" Meg asked. "I hate being alone with these two."

"Oh, please, Meaghen." Helen looked shaken by her comment. "Enjoying an afternoon with your family is not that bad."

"Kids," Frank joked, checking his cell phone messages. "They're never happy."

"How's Axl doing? He seemed pretty shaken up yesterday. Not that I could blame him. I was upset and, well you know… Pearl being his girlfriend and all."

"What—" Helen started to say.

"I guess you haven't heard," Juniper said, "It's really dreadful, actually. I went to see Pearl yesterday and Axl was there—"

Helen snorted.

"And when I got to her house, she was… dead."

Helen gasped and clasped her hands over her mouth.

"Dead?" Frank said, looking up from his cell phone.

"No way," Meg said in a derisive tone.

"What… What happened?" asked Frank, wrapping his arm protectively around his daughter. He looked a little green around the gills.

"She was killed. Stabbed to death, I think."

The family stared at Juniper, dumbstruck.

"I… That's stunning," Frank said. "What a terrible thing. You found her?"

Juniper nodded. "Sort of. Axl arrived right before me. Didn't he tell you?"

"What? No. We went and picked up Meg from University. She lives there and we haven't seen him for a few days. He doesn't sleep at home all the time. Wow…" Helen trailed off, blew out a breath. "I can't believe this. I spoke to her just the other day. Who would have done such a thing? And why? Have the police been called?"

"Yes, of course," Juniper said.

"I suppose they'll be visiting us soon, then. Oh, my dear," Helen said to her daughter. "You feel it, don't you?"

Frank cleared his throat.

"Well, well," Helen said, looking around as though summoning strength from the cosmos. "I imagine Pearl is in a better place now—enjoying a cup of tea in the garden with Kaitlyn."

Meg's face was ashen, and Juniper saw tears in her eyes. She looked away and cleared her throat. "I'm gonna go wait in the car," Meg said, heading down the street.

"Meg?" Frank shuffled after her.

"You didn't have a chance to talk to her at all, then?" Helen asked.

Juniper shook her head. "I arrived after the… it had happened."

"I didn't realize you knew her well," Helen said.

COOKIES, CORPSES AND THE DEADLY HAUNT

Juniper shrugged, not wanting to mention that she had reached out to Pearl only because she was looking into her daughter's death.

"Well," Helen said, blowing out a breath and standing straight, as though to shrug off her uncharacteristic show of emotion. "I guess we should go find Axl and make sure he's alright. Nice to see you, Juniper," she said and walked in the direction of her family.

TWENTY-ONE

U p on the old widow's walk, Juniper couldn't help but think of her encounter with the neighbor yesterday, something about what she said was bugging her. The Halloween Ball was tonight and the thought of the ghost or Peter appearing made her shiver.

Her gaze followed the horizon. Why was the ghost always up on the hill? What was drawing her up there?

Once Jack left, Juniper went back to the second floor, where she'd heard the music yesterday. According to the discrepancies between her measurements and the blueprints, Juniper was sure there was space behind this wall. But... could it be something more? Something that would account for the music and the other noises—whispering, a man yelling—she'd heard? The easiest way to find out was to peek behind one of the sconces but she didn't want to do any damage. She unscrewed one, pulled it from the wall, removed the plastic electrical box, and stood on her tiptoes, trying to shine her flashlight beam in the small hole.

"Lose something?" a voice from behind her said.

Juniper squeaked and flailed as she whirled around.

"Sorry," Cody said with a smile. "Absorbed in thought?"

"Yes, actually," Juniper stood back and handed him the flashlight. "You're taller than I am. Look in there and tell me what you see."

He peeked in.

"There's nothing but empty space," he said, rearing back from the wall a little and looking surprised.

"That's what I thought." Juniper turned and began pulling and tugging at things around the room.

"What are you looking for?" Cody asked.

"The entrance to a secret passage."

"A secret passage? Seriously?"

"I think maybe you've read one too many mystery novels."

Juniper ran her flashlight beam along all the seams, looking for a trigger. "There has to be a way to get in there?"

"You're a contractor, why don't you just punch a hole through.

"I could but old-style lath and plaster is tough and besides I don't want to make a mess for tonight."

Then Juniper turned her attention to the bedroom across the hall—the one with the original bookshelf. It stood about seven feet tall and five wide, and it was set back so the front of the shelves were flush with the wall. Made of what looked like solid mahogany, its ample shelves were fronted with old brass trim.

"The bookshelf is so obvious, but it's cliché for a reason, I guess."

Juniper ran her hand along the spine of the ancient tomes. Pulling on each book, one at a time.

"Hey, one of the books is missing?"

"Really. Which one?"

"There was a book right here on the history of the town. I remember it because I was planning to come back and see if there was anything about the house in it. I got busy and forgot."

"Maybe Jack has it?"

"No, it's not really Jack's thing. I normally do the historical research. He's the hands-on-guy. Do you hear that?" Juniper asked.

Cody nodded. "Classy joint."

"It's coming from the attic.

Their eyes met for a long moment. Then, as though of one mind, they raced for the attic stairs.

"There's nothing here," Cody said when their search proved fruitless.

The music continued, growing louder. Ta da da dan, dan, daaaan…

Juniper ran her hand along the wall seams. "I got nothing either."

"Wait a minute. I think I remember something." Juniper raced into the servant's quarters with Cody closely in tow. "There was a rug right here on the attic floor when I toured the house. After Kaitlyn's murder, you or rather the police took the rug as evidence," Juniper dropped to her knees, "and I remember thinking the floorboards looked like they'd been cut or replaced."

Juniper pulled a carpenter knife from her pocket and ran it along the floor then she wiggled it and it moved. Their eyes met as Juniper lifted a trapdoor.

"What do you know?" Cody commented.

Cody helped her set the removable floor aside. The strains of the orchestra were louder now, clearly emanating from deeper in the dark passage.

"Now what?" He asked.

"We explore."

"You wait here," Cody said. "I'm going to check it out."

"As if I would allow you to go in there by yourself," Juniper scoffed. "This is my house, Detective."

Juniper turned on her pocket flashlight and led the way.

The passage was narrow, only a couple of feet wide. But there were surprisingly no cobwebs, which meant someone had used it other than the ghost. Still the air was musty, and Juniper coughed several times while they made their way along the tiny passageway, following the sound of the music until the passage split in two directions. Cody shone his flashlight down the passage to the right, then to the left. He shrugged.

"Eenie, meenie, miney, moe," Juniper chanted and went to the left. They walked for another minute before coming to a wall.

"It's a dead end."

"That's weird. It's like the Winchester House."

A decoy, I guess. They turned back and this time they went the other way at the fork. They descended a narrow flight of stairs to a small landing where the passage came to an abrupt end.

The detective cast his light around the walls and ceiling, but there didn't seem to be any way out. Juniper recalled the neighbor saying her daughter had seen the ghost in their carriage house. Is that where they were?

While Juniper was pondering this, Cody opened the barn style doors and Juniper realized she was correct.

"Why did the music stop?" Juniper whispered.

"Maybe the ghost is gone."

"Or maybe it's on a timer set by Kaitlyn's killer."

"Sounds like you're going to need an undercover police presence tonight at the party."

"No, I don't think that's necessary." Juniper stopped to think about what she was saying. With secret passages and Peter on the loose, she'd be stupid to refuse help. "Yes, okay, maybe it would be a good precaution, in case, you know, he chooses to return to the scene of the crime."

Juniper glanced at her cell phone. She was due to meet Pike at Cookies & Corsets to get ready for the ball at six, maybe she could squeeze in a meeting with that woman from the historical society before then. She had some questions about this carriage house and she wanted to know what was in that missing book.

TWENTY-TWO

T he woman from the historical society was waiting for her at a table in the back corner of a coffee shop in the next town over; Juniper recognized her from the website. She was a well–put together, somewhat tight-lipped woman. Sixtyish, silver white hair. Attractive in that Helen Mirren way.

"Hi," she said as Juniper approached. Her eyes slid up and down Juniper's outfit. She probably wasn't use to women in work boots.

"Hatti? I'm Juniper. Good to meet you."

"You're the new owner of the Doctor's House?"

"Yes. I'm also a professional historic home renovator, hence the work attire."

Hatti nodded, and they ordered coffee.

"So, what can you tell me about the Doctor's House?"

"What do you want to know," she said as she stirred cream and two packets of sugar into her cup. "Gorgeous property, it was built in 1898 by Doctor Albert Downey for his lovely bride Victoria as a wedding present. The Doctor wasn't from here but Victoria's family owned the local saw mill."

"I had heard that. I'm wondering if there was ever mention of a secret passage?"

"It was quite common to have hidden passages for the servants in those days, so their very well could have been. The Vianu's house, for example, was built around the same time and it certainly does."

"What about the carriage house that sits next door—did it used to belong by chance to the house?"

"Why yes it did, it was all one property that was severed back in the 1960s—I believe that was when the other house sold. The house next door to you—Fern and David Baron—that house was actually built for Victoria's sister Marjorie and her husband, Almer."

"I heard they were the ones who found Albert and Victoria's bodies."

"Yes, so tragic. I couldn't imagine finding my sister like that."

"Is it true Almer hanged himself in my foyer?"

"I'm afraid it is. They were upon desperate times and no one would buy the house. When the town's fire took the saw mill...well, it was the last straw, I guess."

"Did you hear about what happened to Kaitlyn Patone?" Juniper asked.

"Oh! Oh yes, I did. I could scarcely believe it when I read it in the paper!"

"And now Pearl's met foul play too. Did you know Pearl?"

"I did. It's a small town, dear. I know most everyone." Her blue eyes settled on Juniper. "Oh, wait. Are you thinking there was a connection between Kaitlyn and Pearl and the Doctor's murder-suicide?"

"I don't know. I just find it odd that Kaitlyn was murdered in that house and then Pearl was murdered after I started asking her questions."

"Oh, good heavens." Hatti sighed and began shaking another packet of sweetener in the air. "Danger does seem to follow you then. Perhaps it was a mistake for me to meet with you."

Hatti glanced nervously around and then ripped and poured the third packet of sweetener into her mug and stirred vigorously.

Juniper took a gulp of her black coffee, then set the mug down on the table. "Look, I didn't mean to scare you. I'm just looking for answers. There was a book written on the history of the town that was on the bookshelf upstairs. I noticed it's missing. You don't by chance have another copy, do you?"

"No." Hatti glanced around once more than bit her lip. "I do have this." She pulled a file out of her leather satchel. Doctor's House was written at the top in a round, loopy script.

"It's the old photos and archives you asked for," she said. As she opened the file, several photographs fell out. Similar to the sepia-toned photo Juniper had seen at Lulu's house except these were laminated.

Leaning across the table, Juniper picked one up.

"That was Victoria." Hatti said.

She was a pretty, clearly pampered woman with a sad expression on her face. Her hair was obviously long but had been pinned up, she carried a parasol and wore a hoop skirt, gazing over her shoulder at the photographer.

"It's sort of… wistful, isn't it?" asked Hatti.

"Does anyone know why he killed her?" Not that Juniper fully believed that the spirit of this woman lived at the house, but if she did, then it would be good to know her history. "Was there any speculation?"

Hatti looked surprised. "I really have no idea."

"There were no clues?"

"There could be. I believe there was a diary passed down through the family, but you'd need to speak to Lulu about that. That's why I didn't want to meet at Cookies & Corsets. I thought it would be tacky to discuss in front of Lulu." Hatti handed her a photo. "Here they are here."

In the photos there were two little girls standing on the widow's walk. There was also a ghostly, barely there figure in the window behind them, hard to make out against the reflection of the glass.

"Is that the ghost of Victoria?" Juniper asked, pointing to the figure.

"That looks like their grandmother," Hatti said pulling a pair of glasses from her purse. "She owned the house and passed it down to Lulu when she died. They were all very close."

Juniper looked at the photo again and took another sip of coffee. "Who is the other girl? Does Lulu have a sister?"

"No, no that's her cousin, you know Helen."

"Yes, of course. So, you called Pearl the day she died. I saw your name flashing on her cell phone when I found her."

"Oh, how awful! That's when it happened. My god," Hatti said with a little gasp. "What a shock. I almost went over there… how terrible!"

"I know," Juniper said with a little nod. "I wanted to ask you why you had called, and if you knew anything about her schedule that day?"

Hatti shook her head. "The police contacted me about that already. It was nothing, really. As you know Pearl works—pardon me—worked part-time with me. I was just calling her about a project."

"Who was the project for?"

"I'm not really at liberty to discuss other clients."

Juniper counted to three in her head, doing her best to control her temper.

"This is important Hatti. You're nervous and hiding something. I can tell. Who are you afraid of? Peter?"

"That's absurd," Hatti said.

"You can tell me or I can call Detective Lumos," Juniper said finally. Much as Juniper hated to strong arm her, it needed to be done.

"I think Pearl may have stolen the book you were talking about." Hatti blurted. "She called me that morning to tell me about it. She said she'd found it—she didn't mention anything about stealing it."

Juniper nodded.

"So, do you know where it is?"

She blushed and looked away.

"Hatti?" Juniper urged. "Do you have it?"

"Don't be absurd." She checked her phone and then chewed on her lip, in what Juniper was beginning to think was a nervous habit. "It's… in the mail."

"Like in her mailbox, you mean?"

"Would you like a refill?" The waitress said, appearing at the table.

"No, we're almost done." Hatti replied.

After a beat, Juniper said, "Well?" Her words had a subtle edge.

Hatti's eyes watched the waitress walk back to the counter. Then she turned back to Juniper and blushed prettily and shrugged. "She said she mailed it to the historical society because she felt like it was important and she knew someone was after it."

Juniper gave her a tight smile.

"So, you should have it in a day or two?"

She made a grunting sound of agreement and checked her phone. "Are we done here? I need to take my grandchildren out trick-or-treating."

"I'm sorry, yes of course."

And with that Hatti excused herself, leaving Juniper sitting alone, more worried than ever.

TWENTY-THREE

P ike and Juniper met at Cookies & Corsets to don their costumes for the ball. Lulu helped them lace their gowns but left shortly after. With all that had happened she wasn't up for the party and had plans to visit her daughter out of town instead. She said Helen had offered to take her. Juniper couldn't really blame her. From what she'd heard the town loved a good party, and that would make for a lot of nosy people asking Lulu questions.

By the time they'd locked up the shop and crossed the street for the Doctor's House, Lulu's car was long gone.

"We did a good job with those decorations!" Pike said.

The front porch was swathed in one giant spiderweb, complete with creepy egg sacks just starting to hatch. Ghostly figures fluttered across the lawn suspended by fishing line while an eerie orange glow emanated from the windows behind.

The event looked sold out and there was actually a line-up to get in.

They made their way up the porch steps, jostled by a rowdy group of partygoers ranging in costume from classic spooky to fancy Victorian. At last they made it to the front door, showed their tickets and peered into the netherworld of black light, jack-o'-lanterns, and eerie church music that was interspersed with creaking doors and werewolf howls.

They pushed their way through assorted ghouls, goblins, and ghosts to reach the stairs. Earsplitting screams emanated from the upstairs Attic haunt.

As they walked up the curving steps, a girl of about fourteen pushed passed them almost crying.

"I think the haunt is a success," Pike whispered. "It's too bad Jack had to go out of town, all this work and he's missing it."

"I know, but our income property had a plumbing issue. It's not something that can wait. Hopefully he'll get back before it ends."

"I'm gonna go up and try out the attic. Do you want to come?" Pike asked.

The screaming had been constant for the last three minutes.

"No, I think I'll wait right here for you."

"Suit yourself," she said, heading up the stairs.

Juniper walked through the smaller bedroom and out onto the interior balcony that overlooked the landing where the floor-to-ceiling stained glass window looked out over the back of the property. This haunted house was full of people pretend fiends; hopefully Peter wasn't hiding among them.

A streak of white dotted the landscape.

Was that the woman in white wandering up the hill? She could have sworn it was Lulu in her frilly white lace dress. She'd only been in the light for a moment but her dark hair had been teased and wild.

TWENTY-FOUR

J uniper hurried down the stairs and out the back door. The cool night air was fragrant with eucalyptus and damp earth. The fog had rolled in, lending an eerie vibe to the night.

A girl leaned against the house smoking a cigarette. She must have been in her twenties—young, but not a child. And apart from the red hair, she looked a lot like her mother.

"Hi. Sorry. I didn't mean to disturb you," Juniper said.

She shrugged. "Whatever."

"You must be our neighbor, Kara? Fern's daughter?"

"Yeah. Who are you?" She said dropping the cigarette butt quickly and squishing it with her foot. It was clear her family didn't know she smoked.

"I'm Juniper. My partner Jack and I just bought this house." She looked at the worry on Kara's face. "Don't worry—I won't tell."

"Oh thanks! I'm old enough but they wouldn't approve. I come over here to get away sometimes. So, you bought this place, huh? Why?"

"We flip houses for a living."

"How do you flip a house?" Kara rolled her eyes and made a rude noise.

"Sorry… construction term."

She shrugged again, unimpressed.

"We buy old houses and fix them up and then sell," Juniper began, but trailed off as she saw the look of utter boredom on the young woman's face. "Never mind."

"No one is going to want to buy this one. Trust me."

"Why's that?"

"It's haunted…" Juniper could have sworn Kara blushed a little. But the sullen mask descended, and she shrugged. "There's a white lady who roams the place at night. It's pretty creepy."

"So, you've seen the ghost?" Now was Junipers chance to get the details, just in case Peter McCloskey wasn't the perpetrator. "What does she want?"

"How should I know?"

That made Juniper wonder why ghosts couldn't just help solve the crimes perpetrated against them. "Well, do you know what she looks like?"

"She wears a white dress. It's always dark, so it's hard to see anything other than that. Her hair is dark though 'cause I mean if it were light then I would notice. I see her in the upstairs windows sometimes. Pretty much every Tuesday and Saturday night—it's creepy. Anyway, I gotta go."

Juniper watched her leave. She was clearly still in an awkward phase, and she decided maybe she was younger than she'd initially thought: late teens or very early twenties. Juniper remembered that age well. That was when she had been dazzled by the man who later became her boyfriend, Jack Young, the wild young man who worked for her dad.

Speaking of whom… Jack was no longer so young or so wild, but Juniper sure wished he would hurry up and get back. Even assuming Kaitlyn's killer was in the wind, there was a lot of tension in this big old house. Creepy tension.

Juniper was utterly absorbed in her thoughts when she heard an odd sound.

A banging noise. Like metal hitting rock. She listened harder. Was that the sound of dirt being shoveled?

She backed up against the house into the shadows. The sound was coming from the other side of the bushes at the top of the hill.

She took a swig from her punch to build up her courage and contemplated strolling up there. The moon was shining brightly and she could almost make out a motion through the trees.

Was someone there? Or had she imagined it?

Were the ghosts wandering the property in addition to the house, looking for bodies to bury… Get a grip, Juniper, she chided herself. She was going to have to stop listening to those teenager's ghost stories.

There it was again: a flicker illuminating the tree. She saw the glow of yellowish light, as though from a candle, or a flashlight.

"Pretty, isn't it?" came a voice from behind her.

Juniper jumped a good six inches and dropped her glass, which clattered loudly on the tiles as it sprayed its contents across the terrace. She swore a blue streak as she crouched to pick it up.

"Sorry," Fern said with a chuckle. She held out her glass of punch to Juniper. "Here. Have mine."

"No, it's okay…" Juniper looked up at the hill. The light was gone…

"I was checking out the party. That attic is amazing. I thought I was having a heart attack when the man in the mask swung down over the stairs. You need a disclaimer on that attic door."

Juniper laughed.

"I thought I saw my daughter wander this way," she muttered. "She thinks we don't know that she smokes back here."

"Oh, um, yes, I saw her, but she walked around the side with Axl and some others," Juniper said.

Fern let out a mirthless chuckle. "She's extremely sullen, with few social inclinations."

"She was telling me about the ghosts. Do you think she's really seeing them?"

She shook her head. "I don't know. I've never seen them but, then again, I don't look for them. I've seen her after she says she's seen the woman in white and I can tell you, I've never seen her more terrified."

"Hmm, I can relate. I'm beginning to wonder if I'm seeing things."

"What do you mean?"

"Well, this is going to sound crazy, but I saw the lady in white before you came out. Only I think it was Lulu in her costume."

"I thought Lulu was going to her daughter's place?"

"She was supposed to. I'm kind of worried about her."

TWENTY-FIVE

Digging into her purse, Fern pulled out a mini flashlight and headed in the direction of the hill. "Let's go see if we can find her then."

Juniper's heart raced at the idea but she wound through the trees, doing her best to keep up. As much as she didn't believe in ghosts, the thought of them now bothered her.

"Fern, do you always carry around a flashlight?"

Fern laughed. "It's attached to my keys which happened to be in my pocket—a Christmas present from the hubby. I also got safety goggles one year."

"Oh man. Not a great gift giver, huh?"

Lifting the flashlight a few feet, she walked a few more paces and stopped, then flashed the light back and forth in front of them. The bench that had seemed so friendly and inviting only a few days earlier took on a dark and foreboding air.

"Lulu?" Fern called out.

A movement to Junipers left set her teeth on edge. Fern whipped the light around and Juniper sighed when she realized it was only a chipmunk scurrying up a great pine that looked like it had been there for centuries.

"Let's go back. I obviously imagined things earlier."

Juniper's heart was beating so loudly she wondered if Fern could hear it. Surely, she could hear her raspy breath.

A movement to their right caught Fern's attention once again, and she wheeled the flashlight around.

"Another squirrel?" she whispered.

Fern rushed ahead of Juniper a few feet. When Juniper made it to where she was squatted down, she realized she was shining the light on a shovel that had been stuck in the dirt.

She tried to push away the heavy feeling of doom that was growing in the pit of her stomach. Her eyes refused to accept the sight.

They'd found a body.

TWENTY-SIX

"Peter?" Juniper whispered, saying a little prayer under her breath. His body was crumpled on the ground and there was blood crusted to his forehead.

Juniper pulled her cell phone out of her handbag to call the detective. The battery was dead. "Do you have a cell phone," she asked. "We need to call for help!"

Fern reached into her own pocket and shook her head. "Shoot, I must have left it in my purse."

"Okay, let's not panic," Juniper said, clearly on the verge of panicking. "This isn't a horror movie, and we aren't stuck out in the woods somewhere. We'll go back inside and borrow a phone."

"What about Axl and my daughter?" Fern said. "You said they were wandering around back here. What if... I dunno? What if they go after him?"

"They,' who?" Juniper asked.

"The Doctor and his wife? Whoever did that to Peter?"

"Oh Lord, let's go find a phone. Do you think there's any chance he's still alive?"

Fern bent down, "I don't feel anything but the Detectives inside, let's go find him."

"You're right."

Juniper ran toward the house, Fern hot on her heels.

The back terrace was quiet. They raced to the bottom of the hill just as Helen Patone was coming out of the back door.

"Helen," Juniper said, completely out of breath. "What are you doing here? I thought you were taking Lulu to her daughter's?"

"I was supposed to but I haven't been able to find her. I figured she was here. What's the matter? You look upset."

Juniper looked back at the bushes. "Have you seen the Detective? It's an emergency."

She reached out to touch Juniper. "You're shaking. Is someone chasing you?"

"We're fine, but we found Peter."

"Peter? Well, good…"

"Where is he?" Axl stepped from around the side of the house. He had a wild look in his eyes.

Juniper had to stifle a scream. She took a step back.

"He'll pay for what he did to Kaitlyn."

Fern shook her head. "I think he already has."

Juniper grabbed Fern by the wrist and tugged her, "I'm sorry, but we really have to go and find the Detective."

TWENTY-SEVEN

The clouds hid the moon as if it were going to rain, making the night black and foreboding. There was an otherworldly feeling enveloping the yard, all search lamps focused on the dirt pile.

"He still has a pulse!" I heard one of the officers say. "It's faint. Probably been in these woods for a few days now."

One of the younger policemen spoke into his police radio and then walked Juniper around the house while emergency personnel fussed over Peter. There were several people huddled together, Juniper, Pike, Eve, Fern, Axl and Helen. An officer took them one by one and asked the same questions, in different ways, over and over. Juniper's eyelids had that scratchy, heavy feeling that comes with sheer exhaustion. Finally, he took Fern aside.

"This is not where I envisioned Peter running off to," Pike said, taking another sip of her beer as they stood by and watched the mysterious scene.

"You can say that again," Juniper agreed. "It's also not how I envisioned the Halloween Ball."

"Do you think we can leave soon? I really want to get to the hospital."

No sooner did she utter the words than a policeman came over.

"Pike? Detective Lumos would like to speak with you now," he said. "Follow me," he said.

Juniper and Eve were chatting on a bench while the detectives questioned Pike and Fern separately when they noticed Helen mumbling to herself. "I can't believe she really did it. I just can't believe it. I should have believed her."

"Believed what, Helen?" Juniper asked, perking up.

Helen's face went blank like she hadn't realized she'd spoken out loud. "Nothing. I don't know anything. I don't know where Lulu went."

Eve furrowed her brows at Juniper. It was late by now, and the partygoers had started to wander up the hill in ghoulish curiosity. Juniper recognized a few faces but none of them were Lulu.

Juniper tried again, "Helen, do you think Lulu attacked Peter?"

"I'm sorry. I need to find someone." Helen turned and ran off, leaving Juniper and Eve wondering what had just happened.

Part of Juniper felt guilty for all the bad thoughts she'd had of Peter recently. He may have been a bad husband, but he didn't deserve to be hurt and left for dead. She wondered what Pike was thinking. Did she suspect Lulu as well? Had Lulu hurt Peter? Had she killed Kaitlyn?

Juniper didn't have a chance to think about anything else before she felt a hand on her shoulder.

"Officer," she said with a nod.

"Ms… ?"

"Palmer. Juniper Palmer."

"Yes."

"Detective Lumos would like to speak with you now," he said. "He's out front."

Juniper followed him to the driveway where she met Detective Lumos.

"Looks like your house is a crime scene again. Where's your partner?"

"He got called out of town. One of our other properties sprung a leak."

"You own other properties?"

Juniper nodded. "There's not nearly as much murder happening there."

There was a rustle in the crowd of onlookers and Juniper noticed Helen trying to make her way through.

"I said I need to speak to Detective Lumos right now!"

"Come on, please don't make trouble for me, Mrs. Patone. Just wait your turn," the uniformed officer said. "You're up next, anyway. Just wait until he's done."

Helen broke through the imaginary line everyone else was observing. A different police officer tried to shoo her back.

"No, I mean it. It's important I speak to the officer in charge," she said. "I know who hurt Peter!"

A murmur arose from the crowd, and onlookers started voicing their opinions.

Detective Lumos straightened, fixed the crowd with his take-no-prisoners gaze, and then lowered—rather than raised—his voice. "Bring her over."

He turned back to Juniper, muttering, "I'm going to speak with Helen now. You can take Pike to the hospital. I know she's eager to see if Lulu's there."

Juniper nodded and walked away, although she couldn't resist turning back. She couldn't help but wonder just what Helen was up to.

TWENTY-EIGHT

The door to the emergency room opened, and a doctor walked out. Pike, Eve and Juniper stared at him, and Juniper was pretty sure they were all holding their breath.

"I'm Dr. Cider. Are you here for Peter McCloskey?" he asked.

Helen barged through the doors and marched up to the group.

"Yes," Pike said. "Is Peter all right?"

"Are you family?"

"Yes," she said, lying proficiently. "He's our Uncle."

The doctor eyed Helen and Eve, who were clearly too old to be Peter's nieces, and frowned.

"I'm his sister-in-law," Helen clarified.

"I'm the youngest niece," Eve said, daring him to challenge her.

"He's stable," Dr. Cider said, relenting. Thankfully, he recognized a losing battle when he saw one, "he's slipping in and out of consciousness. He has a concussion, and there is another injury—a clean removal of the tissue."

Helen gasped. "What does that mean?"

"A bullet would account for this. It's consistent with other flesh wounds I've treated."

"Oh my God. How could she?" Her knees buckled, and she started to slip to the floor, but Juniper and Eve caught her before her knees hit the tile.

"Stop jumping to conclusions," Pike said as she righted Helen. "What caused the concussion?"

Dr. Cider shook his head. "Until Mr. McCloskey is able to tell us, I can't say. My best guess is that he was struck in the head at some point and shot."

"Or maybe he hit his when he was shot…" Helen suggested.

"Perhaps," Dr. Cider agreed, "but given some other details, I'm not ruling out the possibility that someone struck him on the back of the head. Held him and took him to another location only to shoot him later."

"Good Lord," Helen said. "You think he's been held captive, too?"

Helen started to wobble again and Eve poked her in the ribs. "If you buckle, you'll be the next one with a concussion."

Helen straightened up and shot Eve a dirty look.

"We're keeping a close watch on him for now," Dr. Cider said, ignoring the exchange. "If you're sticking around for a while, I'll pop back in and update you if there are any changes."

Pike reached out to shake the doctor's hand. "Have you seen his wife yet?"

Dr. Cider frowned. "No, the police said they haven't located her yet. I'll tell her you were in and asking about her if I do see her." He gave them all a nod and left.

Juniper looked over at Pike, a sliver of fear running through her. "Where is Lulu?"

"I don't know but she didn't do this," Pike whispered. "She'll turn up."

"You sure about that?" Helen chimed in.

"Yes, I absolutely am. She's a good person. She wouldn't hurt a fly."

Lulu did seem awfully gentle but anyone could be violent if they were cornered. Surely Pike knew Lulu best of all, then again, Helen was family and she seemed to doubt her cousin's innocence.

"Are you going to stick around here?" Juniper asked Pike.

"Yeah, I think Lulu will come here once she finds out what happened to him. Besides, someone has to be with Peter. Lulu wouldn't want him to be alone."

"I have to go," Helen said suddenly.

"Wait," I called out, but she darted down the hall and through the hospital doors before I could finish my sentence.

Eve nodded. "I'll stay with Pike. You go see what Ms. Thang is up to."

Juniper hurried out the parking lot but Helen had already disappeared. What was she up to? Juniper thought the situation over—Helen definitely knew more than she was letting on. She'd need to think up an excuse to go over there.

TWENTY-NINE

The Patone's house smelled of pumpkin and bacon. It was an odd combination, but it made Juniper's mouth water. Inside, Helen hovered in the doorway, a stained apron tied around her waist, eyes swollen and red from crying. A girl with brown hair and a plump figure, the spitting image of Helen, pushed passed Juniper and headed for a small blue car parked in the drive.

"Here's your Tupperware back. I just wanted to say thank you for all your help with the party and for the spooky treats you made. The bat wings were a real hit."

"It was my pleasure. Cooking keeps my mind off things."

The phone rang.

"Please take a seat in the kitchen. I'll just be a moment." Helen motioned to her left but scooted down the hall.

Juniper perched on a stool at the counter where the contents of the refrigerator seemed to be on the counter, a dozen eggs, bacon, and milk. A few remaining pieces of bacon still sizzled and popped in the huge old iron skillet.

It sounded like she was talking to the police — probably to do with Peter.

She returned and began putting things away.

"Don't mind my daughter, Meaghen. She's been staying with us, because of… well, since Kaitlyn's murder. She wasn't happy with us about insisting that the Haunted Halloween Party go on."

"I understand. Your family's been through a lot," Juniper said, suddenly regretting her decision to drop by. Helen seemed overwhelmed.

"We'll be all right…" She hesitated, and the phone rang again.

"It's okay. Please answer it."

She hurried from the room again but this time Juniper couldn't make out the conversation because she was whispering. Juniper wandered out into the foyer admiring the family photos along the wall—awkward middle school pictures of all the Patone kids. There was even a shot of Lulu and Peter with the Patones. Meaghan's hand rested on her mother's shoulder while Kaitlyn's rested on Lulu's. The set-up reminded Juniper of the old sepia photo Lulu had stolen from the house—the one of the doctor and Victoria with her sister, Marjorie, and her family."

"Isn't that a beautiful shot of the family?" Helen's eyes filled with tears. She took a deep breath and blew it out, seeming to regain her composure. "Lulu was so happy then. I wish she would turn herself in. I just know it wasn't her fault that she shot Peter. You don't know Peter like we do."

Juniper thought of the day she'd seen Helen slap him. She wanted to ask her what they'd been arguing about but that was the job of the police. The less, Juniper involved herself in, the better.

Helen stuck out her chin, then frowned. "He was quite abusive, and he was always threatening to put her back in the mental institution—a monster, really." Helen went on. "I still think Peter was the one who killed Kaitlyn, no matter what that officer said… but I have no proof. I bet Lulu lost it when she realized he seduced my poor baby girl and killed her." She started to tear up. Juniper saw a Kleenex box on one of the tables and got one for her. "Kaitlyn was like a daughter to Lulu. I'm sure she had one of her mental breaks and Peter's shooting was probably an accident that she had to cover up."

"Where do you think she would go? Do you think she'll hurt anyone else… if you don't mind me asking?"

"Really, I don't mind. In fact, it's nice to have someone to talk to. I was just having some tea."

Juniper followed her and took seats in a comfortable, overcrowded living room. On the broad coffee table sat a plate of baked goods.

There was a painting over the fireplace of The Doctors House. It was eerie but beautiful.

"Isn't that a beautiful painting?" said Helen joining her.

Juniper nodded and took a seat.

"My great-great-great-grandmother had it commissioned. It was really too bad Peter and Lulu let it fall to waste the way they did. A house like that deserves to shine. It should have been mine. We would have taken care of it. You know I even tried to buy it from them and they wouldn't sell to us. So strange, those two."

"How did Lulu inherit it?"

"Pumpkin cupcakes with maple-bacon icing," she said. "Homemade."

Juniper didn't have to be asked twice. Helen poured the tea.

"Mmm," Juniper said savoring the delicious cream cheese and maple syrup frosting. "This is almost as good as Pike's, but don't tell her I said so."

"It's an old family recipe. My grandmother used to make them every Thanksgiving. You know she used to live in your house. That's how Lulu inherited it."

"Really?" Juniper said, faking surprise. She wanted to hear what Helen had to say.

"She lived there until she was ninety-two, tough old bird." She shook her head and bit into the cake. Crumbs fell onto her large bosom, and she brushed them off with a chagrined smile. "The last ten years of my grandmother's life she began to lose it—kept saying the ghosts spoke to her. My mother and I moved in, to take care of her. Lulu's mother lived on the other side of town and neither one of them bothered much with the family. Eventually my Grandmother worsened, and she turned on us. She was delusional; she was convinced we were stealing her money. She wrote my mother out of the will without my mother's knowledge. It was heartbreaking. We were virtually kicked out, of course by then I'd met Frank and we were dating. It wasn't long after that we married and my mother came to live with us until her death."

"That is a really sad story. I almost feel guilty for buying the house."

Helen got to her feet and switched on the fireplace. Soon, a small but cheerful fire brightened the room. "Now, now, don't feel bad. Why do you think I was so happy when I heard you were buying it? This painting brings me some comfort but I still miss living there. My hope is that once you and Jack are done with the restoration, you'll sell it to me. It should really stay in the family."

Juniper considered this news. They'd been so concerned that no one would buy it. This would solve that problem. "We'd be happy to," Juniper said, smiling. "For a hefty sum."

Helen laughed as I'd hoped she would.

"Money is no object for us, my dear... as you can see. Frank comes from old money. I bet he could even help that business of yours. He has a lot of contacts, you know."

"I think this is the beginning of a beautiful friendship, Helen," Juniper said, sticking out her hand to shake.

"Indeed." She agreed taking it. "Did you want to see the other paintings? I keep those upstairs. One is a striking painting of Victoria before she married. It's a reproduction of an old photo so it's black and white but they've added just a bit of color to her lips. It's so beautiful."

Juniper followed her up the stairs, noticing photos along the wall. Her eyes lit on a family portrait, just like the one she'd seen at Lulu's. She studied the photo. The young woman was lovely, with a cupid's bow mouth, her long hair pinned up in an elaborate bun. But the expression in her eyes was sad, and yearning, and... it felt as though she had something to tell her.

"Is that...? That isn't Lulu's picture of the family, is it?" Juniper asked, thinking it couldn't be. It isn't cracked like Lulu's.

"Oh, no, of course not. That was my mother's. There were two of these taken—one for each of the sisters. Lulu's was passed down from her mother."

"Really, I think there might have been three. There was one at my house but it disappeared."

"No. I don't think so." Juniper followed Helen the rest of the way up the stairs and into the guest bedroom where several oil paintings hung.

"You have your own little gallery collection going on here," Juniper said. "They are quite stunning."

"I know. I can't wait to see them hung once again on the mansion walls."

A thump sounded from the floor above.

"Meaghan's room was turned into a sewing room after she moved out so she stays in the guest suite on the third floor now when she visits."

A muffled voice floated down the stairs… then the sound of glass shattering and more muffled crying.

Helen reached out and squeezed Juniper's arm as she walked her back out of the bedroom. "I'm sorry but she's been having a hard time. She must need me. Kaitlyn's death has been so hard on all of us. Would you mind showing yourself out? We can finish our tour another time."

"Of course, I've intruded on you long enough," Juniper said turning in the direction of the stairs. "Thank you so much for having me." Suddenly, it occurred to Juniper that she'd seen Meaghan leaving earlier.

Her face must have given away her thoughts.

"We have a back door. She probably snuck back in. She doesn't like company."

"Of course."

"Great! Talk to you later," she said and hurried up the stairs to the third floor.

Something about the situation didn't feel right. Wouldn't they have heard Meaghen return? Helen seemed sketchy—she was definitely hiding something. She was so protective of Lulu. Would she harbor a criminal?

There was a crazy amount of thumping going on now. If Lulu was capable of holding her husband captive and shooting him, what's saying she wouldn't hurt Helen in order to escape? Juniper's panic rose with the frenzied noises above and she debated calling the police.

Juniper couldn't in good conscience just walk away and allow Lulu to hurt Helen. On the other hand, Lulu could be arrested and Helen would be furious if Juniper outed her cousin as a criminal. Juniper felt torn. Helen was going to buy the house and help with the business, and then Spirited Construction's money problems would be over. She wouldn't take kindly to Juniper's interference if she had everything in control. Juniper started down the stairs to the main floor but couldn't leave without knowing that Helen was okay. Meaghen's car is probably in the drive. That would put her at ease. Juniper walked to the bathroom window, which could see let out on the main street. No blue car in the driveway. That's when she noticed the white dress that hung inside the shower. It was muddy. Oh god, Juniper was right: Helen was hiding Lulu.

Juniper's fingers hovered over the numbers on her cell. She should call the police but she just couldn't bring herself to betray Helen. Running through her options, Juniper decided instead to send Pike and Jack a text before entering the third floor, deciding that if what Helen said was true, then Lulu was mentally ill and the attack had most likely been an accident.

Juniper climbed the staircase, into the attic-turned-bedroom.

No more banging or yelling.

No Helen, either. Juniper wondered if Lulu had knocked her out…

But then she glanced at the corner and gasped. "Lulu."

Lulu was on the ground, her hands tied behind her back. She was breathing like she was about to hyperventilate, her eyes huge with terror, duct tape covering her mouth. Helen held a gun to her head.

"Helen?" Juniper said quietly. "What's going on?"

"You're going to help me now," she said. She was breathing hard as well. That made three of them. "I'm going to follow you down the stairs and we're going to go get that dress. Go on, now, lead away," Helen continued. "I know you already saw it, you're too nosy not to have."

"I don't know what you're talking about," Juniper said with a shake of her head. "Why are you doing this? You shot Peter?"

She wasn't holding the gun in the way an experienced marksman would. But at this range, lack of skill didn't make a gun any less lethal.

"And don't forget about Kaitlyn," Helen said, perking up. "That self-righteous little witch."

"No way. You killed your own daughter?" Juniper asked, shocked. She had not been expecting that. Lulu began to cry harder. "Please remove the tape on Lulu's mouth, can't you see she's panicking."

Juniper's mind raced. "Poor Lulu." She whispered. She scolded herself. Why hadn't she called the police? She was still close to the stairs, she could run. But what about Lulu—would it mean certain death for her?

"Poor Lulu… It's always poor Lulu," Helen mocked.

"Please tell me Kaitlyn's death was an accident. You cannot be cold blooded enough to murder your own flesh and blood and stuff her in a trunk like that on purpose."

"Of course, it was an accident. I never meant to kill her but she found out the truth."

"What do you mean the truth?"

"Never mind that. I'm not selling my sob story to you but I couldn't let her blab, it would sink me."

"Was Kaitlyn having an affair with Peter? Were you?" Juniper asked point blank.

Helen laughed like I'd just told the funniest joke in the world.

Juniper wracked her brain to understand. She was missing something obvious.

"That was my greatest lie. I can't believe the town believed me. Peter was the most faithful loyal husband I'd ever met. He would never stray on Lulu. He was obsessed with her. Not like that cheating bastard Frank. I put the idea of Peter's infidelity in Lulu's head so they'd fight. Peter was not cooperating with my business designs and I needed Lulu on my side."

Lulu whimpered. Juniper thought about what Lulu had been through, believing her husband had thrown her aside and now hearing he was faithful and knowing he could still die. Or did she think he was already dead? Was she blaming herself now?

"Kaitlyn called her brother for a ride that night. She was in your attic and she found… well never mind what she found." Lulu paused to collect her breath. "It doesn't matter—none of it matters. Her next call was going to be to Lulu and Peter. Axl was busy, thank the lord and so he called me rambling about Kaitlyn being drunk and belligerent in your attic. I told him to never mind that I would take care of it and I went over there. She was drunk and mean and she was ready to expose me. It got heated, and she tripped and hit her head. I had no choice but to set Peter up."

"Why do you need the dress?" Juniper asked.

"Why do you think? The ghost shall strike again."

"The ghost," Juniper said, thinking of the neighbor's story. The ghost appeared on Tuesdays and Saturdays. That was when Helen said she had meetings.

Juniper could see in her peripheral vision that Lulu was working on freeing her hands.

She had to keep Helen talking, to give her time.

"So, you were the one who I saw on the hill the night of the Halloween party? That was some great acting skills, pretending to be shocked that Peter had been shot and then blaming Lulu the way you did at the hospital."

"Brilliant, if I do say so myself. When Lulu told me how she'd showed you the dress—I just knew you'd assume the worst come time. After I ditched the dress, I ran into you and your nosy neighbor. The wig was sticking up out of my purse, I about collapsed afterward when I realized. I thought the gig was up, but I guess you didn't see it."

"No, I didn't. So, what are you planning to do with Lulu?"

"Well I was planning to hold her and eventually have her committed but now you've gone and changed my plans, haven't you?"

"I don't understand."

"Go get the dress and you will. Thing is, Juniper, Lulu was never crazy, not in the way you're thinking. I used to give her psychotic meds that would make her act crazy— so that she wouldn't live in the house, forcing Peter to sell it to me."

"But it backfired. He wouldn't sell you the house, would he?"

"No. He was protecting his crazy wife—thought she wouldn't get any better until it was out of the family and off limits for her to visit." Helen shook her head and said again, "He was a stubborn man."

Juniper frowned. "You killed Peter McCloskey because he was protecting his wife? You are one cold hearted woman."

Her eyes scanned the room for a weapon. There was nothing close enough. There were some gardening tools, but they were on the other side of the attic. If only Lulu and I were reversed in our positions.

Helen's eyes went flat. She squinted at Juniper and stood straighter like she knew what she was thinking. "I'm just trying to get back what was rightfully mine. Go get the dress. Otherwise, I'm going to shoot Lulu right now and blame it on you. I'm not kidding, Juniper. I'm losing my patience."

"But—"

Lulu broke free, grabbed a shovel against the wall beside her and brought it down, hard, on Helen's instep. She cried out and started hopping around on her good foot. Lulu leaped up and kicked Helen in the kneecap. Her leg buckled, and she crashed to the ground like a sack of potatoes.

Juniper ran toward them, launching herself at Helen when she saw her trying to point her gun. Juniper grunted as she landed on her full force and grabbed for the hand that held the gun. Juniper jammed it into the floor board, and then Lulu, standing over them, stomped on Helen's wrist.

She cried out again and let go of the weapon.

Juniper went for the gun. Lulu went for Helen.

She started yelling, swearing, roaring in rage as she kicked her, landing blow after blow. Blood poured from a broken nose, and a kick to her gut made her double over in pain.

"Help!" Helen yelped, her voice panicky and high-pitched. "Get her off me!"

"Lulu," Juniper said. "Enough. I have the gun."

Lulu continued, landing another blow on Helen's already injured knee. Helen screamed.

"Lulu." Juniper took her by the shoulders and physically drew her away from her cousin. "That's enough."

"But she… she killed my daughter and my husband…"

"Kaitlyn was your daughter?"

Lulu's eyes met Juniper's, huge and solemn, as always. But then she smiled.

"She was, and she was going to tell me! That was the secret." She nodded and tears poured down her face. "She looked just like me, don't you think? I always thought so. I'm not crazy, Juniper. I'm not."

Juniper laughed in nervous relief. "Yes. I know. Let's tie Helen up and call the police."

"They're already on their way," Jack said as he entered the doorway, huffing and puffing. "I called them before I broke the window to get in—I tried texting you back but you weren't responding, and I was afraid you were hurt."

Jack crossed the room and took the gun from Juniper. His hand was bloody from punching through glass. There was a fierce, determined glint in his eyes, but there was something else that Juniper couldn't identify as he locked his gaze on her. Juniper didn't think she could have looked away if she wanted to.

But she didn't want to look away.

He set the gun behind him on a desk and pulled her into him. He's going to kiss me, she thought, and then his lips were on hers and she couldn't form one coherent thought.

It was like the time they'd been remodeling their first house and she'd touched the exposed wires. Except this wasn't a little jolt of electricity. Something sparked when their lips touched and that energy fizzed through every inch of her, all the way down to her wobbly knees.

He lifted his head, and she blinked. There were other things going on...important things, she knew, like Lulu tying Helen up, but at the moment, she didn't care about them. She didn't remember wrapping her arms around him, but she was gripping his shoulders as tightly as she could.

His face looked the same as always, tightly controlled, but there was something about his eyes, a softness, a tenderness that surprised her. "So, I'm confused... why is Helen the one tied up?"

"That's all you have to say?" Juniper said, leaning back against his arms, against the solidness of his hands on her back and shoulders. "After a kiss like that?"

"A kiss should never require explanation," he answered, then his face turned serious. "Junie, I was so afraid."

That caught her off guard. *Jack, afraid?*

"You were?" she whispered.

"I thought I was too late and you're the best friend I've got."

THIRTY

O ne week later, Helen was in police custody and Jack and Juniper stood in the foyer of the Doctor's House, reading over an outrageous offer from their real estate agent, Jack Sr.

The Halloween decorations were gone and now there were only freshly painted paneled walls with ornate moldings. Polished antique crystal chandeliers hung from decorative plaster medallions overhead. It looked lovely and after just one open house, they were sitting on a multitude of offers.

"Dad said the buyers loved the idea of the secret passage," Jack said. "The wife's a writer, and the husband's an architect."

"That's great, Jack. I'm so pleased."

"Spirited Construction will make more money on this one house than we've made from all of our other flips combined."

Juniper nodded, sadly, taking another long look around the room. "We'll have enough to go our separate ways." She could no longer hear the strains of the classical waltz. They had found the wireless speaker that Helen had planted in the ceiling in the dead-end passage so she could scare away potential buyers. "I'm sure Sally will be thrilled to see us dismantle the company."

He shrugged. "Yes. She would love that. Actually, she gave me an ultimatum—her or you."

"I see. Well, I guess this is goodbye then." Juniper held out her hand. Jack took it and pulled her in close for another electrical, toe-sizzling kiss. When he broke away, Juniper's heart was pounding.

"Why must you keep torturing me like this?"

Jack pushed her back but hung onto her arms. His face was deadly serious. "You know, Junie, when I found you in the attic. All I could think about was how empty my life would be if I lost you. You're the best part of my day..." he swallowed.

"You're just figuring this out now," she said lightly. "What about Sally? Does she know any of this?"

"I broke up with her last month." He pushed a strand of hair away from the corner of her eye. "I've been trying to find a way to ask you out," Jack said.

"Are you kidding me? What took you so long?"

"You're kind of intimidating." Jack closed the narrowing distance between their lips and kissed her hard. He pulled away with a muttered curse, "And not the most forgiving of people… besides, every time I turned around that pesky detective was sniffing around. You're not seeing him, are you?"

"Maybe I am."

"He's a really nice guy, but he doesn't really seem like your type…"

"Oh yeah, and what's my type?"

His voice grew faint and husky. "Me… And only me."

THIRTY-ONE

Two days later, Peter had been released from the hospital and Jack and Juniper stood inside the passage that led into the neighbor's carriage house, where Jack was putting on a sliding barrel bolt and Juniper was doing her best to explain Lulu's story—how she'd owned but been tricked into selling the Doctors House and of course how Kaitlyn was her daughter.

"So, Frank was guilty too?" He said, drilling the plate in place.

Juniper waited for the loud whir of the drill to stop. "Well no, not like Helen, but he admitted that she blackmailed him twenty-two years ago and I think he turned a blind eye after that."

He paused and turned to Juniper. "What did Helen blackmail him with and why?"

"According to Helen, who is trying to cut a deal, she caught Frank in bed with Lulu one night, which ultimately resulted in Kaitlyn."

"Lulu and Frank were having an affair?" Jack asked, holding my gaze for a beat.

"No. Helen was drugging Lulu so that she would see ghosts in order to convince her to sell the house. She began to sleep at Helen's house at least once a week. While she was unconscious, Frank decided to hop into bed with her and raped her and Helen caught him."

"When she began to experience morning sickness, Helen devised a plan. She told Peter that she'd caught Lulu seducing Frank and that he admitted they'd slept together once before. She convinced him that it was because of her mental problems and that she'd gone off her meds so she didn't remember and that it would be best for everyone if Frank and her raised Kaitlyn as their own. Peter reluctantly agreed."

Jack looked confused. "What about Lulu? She must have known she had a baby."

They paused while he drilled the other fastener in place. When he was done, Juniper continued on with the story. "Helen paid off the hospital staff and told Lulu the baby died. Helen had been wearing a fake belly so everyone thought she was pregnant too and that she delivered Kaitlyn.

After that, Lulu really did start to have mental issues, whether it was the side effects from the drugs or losing the baby."

"Who wouldn't have? What a screwed up, twisted thing to do to a person." Jack commented.

"I know. Peter had her committed for a month but eventually he felt bad and had her released and, from then on, Helen said he doted on her completely, letting his business fall to the side. That's why they were having money issues."

Jack nodded his head, sighing. "That's too bad. Hey, I found the wires for the sound system in here," he said, shifting on his side and peering into the hole.

"The what?"

"The sound system. You know, it's how she played the music." He pointed at the wire. "Hand me that flashlight."

Juniper kneeled down, reached inside the bag, and pulled out the larger flashlight.

"You look so… manly," Juniper told him.

He smiled at her. "What?"

Juniper grinned. "I dunno. You've got all these tools, and it's very sexy." As soon as Juniper said the word, she bit back a giggle.

"Good to know," he said. "I'll be sure to work with tools, I mean flashlights more often." He straightened and walked down the hall—the one that led to the dead end.

"Where are you going?" Juniper asked. "Are we done putting the lock on this door?"

"Yes," he clarified. "I just want to see where this wire leads to." They walked for a minute until they came to the end of the hall. It was the same dead end that the detective and Juniper had first found. "That doesn't make any sense? It must lead somewhere." He frowned and climbed the ladder until he could push on the roof. Sure enough it moved and light crept in. "Voila. We found the control for the sound system." The dials stared him in the face. He pushed the hatch all the way open. "And another exit," he said, climbing all the way out. "The gardens on the hill."

"Well, I guess we know how she was able to get around."

EPILOGUE

An hour later, they were served pints at the Pub in the next town over. Jack sipped his craft brew, "So, how did you know all those details?"

"Well, some of it Helen rhymed off while she was pointing a gun at me, and some of it the police told me."

"Why would the police tell you anything?"

"I guess I'm making friends here."

"I bet it was that Detective Lumos guy. You better be careful. I think he's got his eye on you."

"Why should I be careful?" Juniper smiled and chewed flirtatiously on her lip, all innocent like.

Jack grumbled.

"I'm teasing. It was because Lulu insisted, I be there when they questioned her, and they told her a lot of it. Oh, and they found our missing book—guess what was inside?"

"What?"

They paused while the waitress returned to offer refills and dropped off the appetizers. There was no point spreading the gossip further; Lulu was going to have enough to live with. When she was gone Juniper continued on with the story. "Kaitlyn's real birth certificate—Peter had hidden it inside the book with a note—I guess he had a feeling he might need it someday. He showed it to Kaitlyn and we think she was planning to confront Helen with it when she killed her. She must have told Pearl about it—or at least told her there was something important inside that book."

Just then the door opened and in walked Pike.

"Well what's the emergency?" She asked, squishing into the booth beside Juniper. "Why did you need me to meet you here ASAP?"

"Take your coat off, order a drink—all in due time," Juniper said, motioning for the server to bring another beer. "Where were you, anyway?"

"Visiting Lulu," she said, stealing a sip of Juniper's beer.

"Junie's been filling me in. What a crazy town this is," Jack teased.

"Tell me about it." She dropped her purse on the floor and it landed with a thud. "What's going on in this place? It used to be so dull and monotonous and... safe. I don't understand. There was a complete soap opera happening under my nose or rather in my shop."

"How is Lulu doing?" Juniper asked.

"She's doing better. They're running some tests to see what sort of long-term effects the drugs Helen was giving her might have had. The things she told me were crazy though. I understand now why Peter was always hovering and calling her and checking up on her. I thought he was controlling, but he was simply worried about her."

"Is she going to be alright, do you think?" Jack asked.

"I think she'll bounce back and I'll be there when she does."

"Well if she doesn't bounce back and you need a place to run your business out of, you could move into the Inn."

"What?"

"Jack and I discussed it and we turned down the real estate offer. We're thinking that maybe this time we're gonna stick around."

"You're going to open an Inn at the Doctors House."

"Yes, only we won't call it that anymore. We've settled on the Gothic Haunt."

She looked down as if only just noticing that Jack and Juniper were holding hands.

"And this thing between you two… it's back on."

Juniper nodded.

"I love it!" Pike shouted, practically spraying her beer on Juniper. "And I'm no expert, but this Inn is going to make so much money. I mean aside from the Caravan, the closest motel or bed-and-breakfast is thirty minutes away. Everyone is always complaining when there's a wedding or a function that there's nowhere for out-of-towners to stay."

"Good. Because we just put in a new kitchen that we're basically going to have to re-do. Sooo… would you want to move your café in? We could make room," Juniper asked again pinching her arm.

Pike's eyes watered. "That's a sweet offer, but I'm good across the road. Lulu is staying whether she likes it or not. I do have another idea though." She eyed the room dangerously.

"Go on," Juniper said, knowing exactly where she was heading.

"What about one of these?"

"A pub?" Juniper asked.

"Yeah, we don't have anything like this in town and I've heard it suggested a few times now at the town meetings but no one has the space."

"I think you're right," Juniper said. "Which is what Jack, and I were thinking. That is, if you didn't want to move in."

"But not a full restaurant like this one, because we don't want that sort of hassle," Jack clarified.

"No," Juniper agreed. "We were thinking more of a taproom, somewhere for the guests to have a drink and a light bite to eat."

"How about tapas," Pike said.

"I love tapas," Juniper agreed. "Of course, if you refuse to partner with us then you may have to teach me to cook or maybe I'll buy a cookbook. Do they still sell those?"

Pike laughed. "That reminds me, I brought you guys a house warming gift. Well, it's not from me… it's from Lulu."

"Seriously?"

She refused to meet Juniper's eyes, but she held out a book that looked to be a hundred years old.

"What in the world is this?"

"Victoria's Diary."

"And you're giving it to me because…?"

"Lulu said it needs to stay with the house. I think she still believes that Victoria really does haunt the place. It might be neat to read it."

Juniper frowned, thinking it over. "I guess it would be interesting. Let's just hope I don't start seeing her."

Thanks for reading *Cookies, Corpses and the Deadly Haunt*.

Keep reading for a sneak peek at book two in the Haunted House Flippers series: <u>Candy Canes, Corpses and the Gothic Haunt</u> where they transform the old Victorian mansion into Bohemian Lake's first Inn & Taproom. Unfortunately, the mansion's poltergeist is out to dash their merriment with mean-spirited sabotage.

ONE

The front door of Cookies & Corsets opened just as Juniper Palmer dunked one of the café's seasonal jolly ginger reindeer cookies into her candy cane latte. Soft, sugary scents wafted into the air as she licked the whipped cream from her lips. Five more minutes and then she'd head back across the road to her Victorian mansion to see how the building inspector had made out. Hopefully, the news would be better this time.

The sound of Christmas carols mingled with the chatter of the café's customers. It was non-stop in Bohemian Lake this time of the morning, which was fantastic for Pike Hart, who owned the café, though it guaranteed her a cold mug of coffee.

"Why, Juniper Palmer. Look at you! Beautiful as always. Come here and see me," Eve Banter said, trotting up to Juniper's table. "And tell me, how's that Ghostly Inn coming along?"

Juniper set her coffee down to address the town's kookiest resident when they were joined by Eve's boss, Penelope Trubble. "It's the Gothic Haunt, Eve."

Juniper smiled to herself. Being a journalist, Penny was a stickler for facts.

"Good morning, ladies," she said as she got to her feet, wrapping an arm around each of them, and pulling them in for a big hug. "It's inspection day, so cross your fingers and toes for me."

"Consider it done. This one will cross her eyes for you too, won't you, Pen?" Eve said with a wink.

Penny rolled her eyes and turned her attention back to the blackboard of specialties.

Eve leaned in. "See, told you."

Juniper didn't bother to explain that crossing and rolling were two different things.

"Anyway, I can't wait for that taproom of yours to open. It'll be nice to have somewhere to go for a drink aside from that dive over by the hardware store."

"You mean Guitars and Cadillacs?" Penny asked, turning back around.

"Heck no, I wouldn't step foot in that place. I meant the alley behind it. It's cleaner! Not to mention, the cats screeching on the fence could harmonize better than the bands Evan Cross hires."

"Eve!" Penny scolded. "Have you no inside voice?"

Eve peeled her fuzzy mittens from her hands and smoothed down her long reddish-brown hair. "I do." Her big, brown eyes were trapped in a perpetual state of amusement. "Of course, it says the same thing as the outside one." She deposited her gloves on Juniper's table and turned to the barista. "Now, Velma. How 'bout you fix me a tipsy cocoa with extra sprinkles?"

"I think not," Penny interjected. "Just the cocoa, Velma, and make it three, please? I certainly don't need a tipsy assistant at the paper. You know what happened last time, Eve."

"Oh, you're such a bah-humbug, Penelope Trubble. I don't know why I allow you to employ me. And anyway, that old man had it coming."

"That old man is my father, and your boss!"

"*Yada, yada.* What is your problem? It was just a little laxative." Eve smirked and turned back to Juniper, pulling open her giant handbag. Inside were several suspicious looking bottles and a giant ring of keys. "Just ignore her, sugar. That's what I do. Anyhow, I brought the tipsy with me. Let's ditch the Cindy Lou and take a stroll down Main Street? What say you?"

An unexpected laugh burst from Juniper's lips just as the door swung open once again, smacking the ladies with an icy burst of wind and snow. Penny zipped her coat back up and grabbed the tray of drinks from the counter. "Come on, Cratchit, back to work we go. Or I'll dock your pay and Tiny Tim will starve."

Eve faked a groan and followed her feisty, red-haired boss out the door with a quick yet overly dramatic wave.

Juniper waved back. The disdain those two pretended to have for each other was all an act, and Juniper enjoyed watching. She'd take them over a comedy show any day.

With the door open, a surly looking man in a red tweed coat slid inside behind a rosy-cheeked couple just as Penny and Eve slid out. Pike's poor barista had just mopped and sat down for her break. The man dashed the toes of his boots against the welcome mat impatiently, leaving little tufts of snow to melt at the threshold.

Juniper felt bad for the barista and was preparing to pitch in when the doors to the back kitchen swung open, and Pike, a cool blonde in a green apron, returned. One oven-mitt-clad hand clutching a tray of chocolate peppermint croissants, the other clutching a steaming mug of tea.

"Good morning," bubbled Pike after she'd delivered the order. She smelled of cinnamon buns and cocoa as she whizzed by and Juniper guessed she was baking in that back kitchen of hers. "What can I get you?"

The rosy-cheeked couple who'd removed their coats revealing similar holiday sweaters, looked over the specialty blackboard, then ordered two eggnog lattes. Juniper couldn't help but notice that the man behind them rudely tapped his boot the whole time until finally they got their order and moved to a booth by the Christmas tree. The scrooge looked familiar, but Juniper couldn't quite place him. She'd only lived in Bohemian Lake for two months now, though she'd visited many times before when she and Jack were dating the first time. Still, two months was long enough to meet people in a small town, especially when you owned the local haunted house.

"Good morning, Evan," Pike said, as she returned to the counter and handed the grumpy man his paper coffee cup and a pastry bag. Juniper had gotten to her feet by this time and gave Pike a nod before handing in her dirty dishes and turning to head out the door.

"What's so good about it?" Juniper heard the man grumble.

"Bye, Junie. Good luck on the inspection," Pike shouted after her.

"Junie." The man uttered her name with disgust. Then he bumped her arm as he pushed past her on the way out the café's front door.

"Well, Merry Christmas to you, too, good sir," Juniper shouted after him.

***

"What do you mean the exhaust line has been cut?" Juniper said. "That's not possible." She paced the dining room floor of her old Victorian mansion, taking in the curved architecture of the room and puzzling over how a house so perfect could be such a headache.

"I'm sorry. I can show you again." He set his jaw and pointed back toward the commercial-grade kitchen they'd just put in. "You're going to have to replace the wiring."

He'd shown her twice already, and he was right. The line running to the brand-new stainless steel ventilation system had been tampered with.

"You're also missing a vacuum breaker on the outside tap. You'll have to schedule another inspection after you get these replaced."

This should have been the final building inspection. It was one thing after another lately—as if the house was out to get them. The opening of her Inn and Taproom—the Gothic Haunt—was just over two weeks away.

"Sign here, please, to acknowledge that you didn't pass."

As the inspector passed a clipboard to her, she watched three of her construction workers moving in and out of the house. They were removing the old metal shelving from the basement. Jack and Juniper had put a temperature controlled wine cellar in last week with all new racks.

The inspector who had previously dealt with Juniper's partner and boyfriend, Jack Young, studied the clipboard. "Juniper Palmer, huh? So, you're Jack's girl from back in the day?"

Juniper nodded to the inspector, thinking of her early twenties. She'd heard the term 'Jack's girl' so often, she'd almost gotten it tattooed across her forehead, even after they'd split up.

Post college—where they'd met through Pike—Jack and Juniper had opened their own company, Spirited Construction. Juniper had still been modeling part-time to help pay the start-up costs and was due to leave on assignment for a month when Jack proposed at his family's Christmas dinner—of all places. In a moment of panic, she had accepted but then turned around and rejected him. They'd broken up and when she'd returned, he was already dating the devil's hand-maiden, Sally Snaub—or Sally Big-Boobs, as Juniper called her. They remained an item for the next four years while he and Juniper maintained a business relationship.

Then they bought this old mansion in October. Jack and Juniper had fallen for the house—ghostly baggage and all—and, much to her own surprise, they'd fallen back in love. Or maybe they'd always been in love and they'd just found their way back to each other. Either way, Sally hit the curb along with the ugly siding that had covered part of the Victorian's brick, and Jack and Juniper began their fairytale dream—or nightmare, depending on which day of this renovation it was.

"Juniper?"

Juniper blinked and looked up. "Sorry. I'm dwelling on what will happen if we don't get this to pass. Everything is all arranged for a New Year's Eve launch."

"Try not to stress too much. Just tell Jack I said to get those things fixed first thing tomorrow, okay, and then give us a call back. We'll do our very best to fit you in," the Inspector said as he left.

Juniper fought the urge to beat her head against the exposed brick wall. What was she thinking, scheduling a big holiday launch without first passing inspection? Thank goodness, Jack was an electrician, but still it would cost them time away from their other projects. Right now, he was staying in the city, working on a Queen Anne restoration. He'd have to come fix this wiring, and then immediately head all the way back to the job site to finish up before the annual Christmas Eve dinner at his parents', which was only a week away. What a colossal waste of time.

Juniper's phone buzzed, and she took a moment to reply to Jack's text about the beam they'd ordered for an open concept farmhouse renovation in the next town over— yet another job that was supposed to be wrapped up before the holidays.

The second Juniper tucked the device back inside her pocket, it buzzed again, and she confirmed an appointment for blown insulation. She'd just ended the call when three of her burly workers fled the basement steps, shouting, white-faced with fear. It would have been comical if she hadn't seen the terror on their faces.

"What is it?" Juniper called out following them. "What's going on?"

Juniper had been in the construction business long enough to know things could go wrong on a job site. "What happened?" she repeated. Now that they were safely on the front porch, they shrugged. She turned around and marched back down the hall to the basement stairs.

"Wait, Junie! Don't... don't go down there!" Juniper heard one of the men yell after her.

Juniper ignored the warning, tromping down the first three steps. As she reached the midpoint on the staircase, she caught a flash of white. The blurry streak had crossed in front of the arched doorway that led into the wine cellar. By the time she realized what she'd seen; the ghost was gone.

"Another problem?"

Juniper started at the sound of the voice coming from behind her.

Her chef, Feliz Merlot. Truth be told, Feliz was more than a chef. He was an old friend from her modeling days. Originally from Spain, he knew just about all there was to know about tapas and wine. He also made the best churros Juniper had ever tasted—not that she'd admit that to her bestie, Pike, who prided herself on being the area's most accomplished baker. Feliz wasn't hard on the eyes, either— muscular, dark hair, and brown-eyed. She'd tried to set him up with Pike to no avail.

"You look like you saw a ghost."

A floorboard creaked. "Very funny, Merlot," Juniper paused. "Upstairs. The vent's electrical wire is faulty. We failed inspection again." Juniper followed him back to the kitchen to show him.

"*Mierda*," he swore. "How?" He ran his fingers through his dark wavy hair and inspected the wire. "Someone did this on purpose."

"But how? No one's been near this kitchen aside from us since it was installed. It probably just broke."

"Wires don't just break. I bet it was that foul-mouthed Louise woman from the cheese shop. She was back here the other day arguing with me, but I don't know when she would have had the chance." Feliz paused as if he was trying to remember.

"Arguing over what?"

"*Queso manchego.* She hates it. Can you believe that—a cheese connoisseur who dislikes the most popular cheese in Spain?"

"Oh, you're being silly, Feliz. People are allowed to have their own opinions and no sane person is going to ruin a business opening over a cheese disagreement."

Feliz shook his head. "Who says she's sane? I don't trust anyone who doesn't like sheep's milk cheese."

"Okay, well, let's just pretend it wasn't the nice lady from across the road. Maybe a mouse chewed it?"

"It doesn't look chewed."

"That's true. I should call Jack. Maybe it was faulty, so he didn't finish hooking it up."

"Does that sound like Jack to you? He wouldn't have left it."

"Maybe he got interrupted?" At this point, Juniper was simply relieved it wasn't something deadly like the gas line.

"*Mierda,*" he swore again.

"There's no other explanation," Juniper said, ignoring the possibility that it had something to do with the ghostly figure she'd just seen. "We're the only ones who have been near it."

Feliz scratched his head. "And what about the half dozen other little things that have gone wrong here the past few months. I'm telling you, *mi amiga*, either it was Louise, or that *espíritu* who lives here is a poltergeist."

This wasn't the first time Juniper had heard his opinion on the matter. Sure, there'd been some minor annoyances, but they'd been bound to happen, especially when dealing with an older home. Jack and Juniper were always running into things like this in the historic home construction business. It went with the territory. Then again, the things that were happening here did seem to be intentional.

"Okay," Juniper said. "So, maybe I don't quite believe these things are accidents." She turned and entered the front foyer. She'd considered bringing in a ghost hunter a couple of weeks ago, a professor of psychiatry and neurobehavioral sciences who just so happened to be the son of a local historian, but she'd decided against it. Perhaps it was time to bite the bullet and reach out. Juniper pulled his card from her pocket and studied the name: Professor Daemon Wraith. It couldn't hurt to get his opinion on things.

She crossed the wide-plank floor of the taproom and sat down at the bar. She refused to believe it was sabotage. This town was full of people who had become family to her. Thirty-five years of neglect had left the run-down Victorian mansion-turned-duplex looking like a haunted house, and everyone was over-the-moon happy that they'd fixed it up.

Feliz took the stool beside her. "*Amiga*, it is no coincidence. Someone is sabotaging us."

"You don't know that," Juniper said. "Everything has been fixable. Don't you think if someone was out to get us, they'd come up with something a little more complex. And how are they getting in? None of the windows have been broken, and none of the doors have been tampered with."

"That means nothing. Perhaps someone stole one of the keys off your friend's massive key ring."

Eve Banter was the unofficial keeper of Bohemian Lake. There was a rumor that she had somehow finagled keys to every business in town. Everyone knew it but nobody really cared.

Juniper laughed. "If there's a person in this town who can outfox Eve, then they deserve that key, but I'll do my due diligence and check with her. Not that she'll ever admit it."

"What about the attic passageway that was used last time to break in and 'fake' haunt you?"

"Jack bolted that sucker up. I saw to that."

"Have you checked to make sure it's still bolted?" Feliz asked.

"No, but good call. I'll do that too."

Feliz stood. "It's dinnertime. Why don't you go home to Jack? I'll lock up tonight."

"Thanks, but Jack is away. He's staying in the city close to the Queen Anne job site. We've reached our deadline, so we can't have the guys slacking off every time we get a dusting of snow."

"Go to the café then and have dinner with Pike. I want to work on that *Natillas de Leche* recipe and I don't need you underfoot, sticking your dirty fingers in my bowls."

"I see. So, you'd rather I poke around Pike's pastries, huh? Well, I'll have you know I only do that for chocolate and, anyway, your custard is delicious already."

Feliz shook his head. "I'm working my churros into it. I want it to have a twist for the big celebration."

If it turned out half as good as the churro, they'd sell out opening day.

Juniper gathered her black leather purse and left a short time later—calling Jack, who promised to be there bright and early in the morning. Once outside, she turned her gaze upward to the mansion's gothic square tower. It was topped by the imposing iron widow's walk and looked stark against the bright gray sky. Sometimes Juniper had to pinch herself. It was hard to believe that, not long ago, this had been a run-down, ghostly shell. The former Doctor's House had been owned by Pike's business partner Lulu McCloskey, but thanks to the poor woman's unscrupulous cousin, the house had been abandoned.

Jack and Juniper had bought the mansion with the intent to flip it but instead they'd fallen for it. They'd cleaned up the Gothic Revival facade, reinforced the widow's walk and patterned shingle roof, and added a commercial kitchen, taproom and dining area, and *voila*, the Gothic Haunt, had been born.

They were now Innkeepers and restauranteurs.

They'd thought about brewing their own beer, but the Bohemian district was filled with wineries and craft breweries, including one run by Jack's own family, so they decided they'd rather work with locals than compete. They were collaborating with the town's council to offer tour packages in combination with the other local restaurants and wineries. Bohemian Lake was already a tourist destination, so why not add to its offerings?

Juniper was tempted to take her chef's advice and drop back into Cookies & Corsets, if only to tell Pike about her inspection, and inquire about the Grinch from earlier, but she was feeling more than a little drained.

Instead, she grabbed a bowl of French onion soup and a sandwich from Deer's Deli and headed for Jack's place. The place was littered with boxes ready to be moved into the attic apartment of the Gothic Inn because what's an Inn without Innkeepers?

They just needed to finish up the cosmetics and they could move the furniture up. That was next up on her to-do list. Speaking of which, with food in her tummy, she set the tub to fill and reviewed the to-do list. By ten o'clock, she was bored. The bath was heavenly, but the unfinished attic was weighing on her mind. It wouldn't hurt to go over to the mansion and plan the layout. There was still so much to be done.

Her phone buzzed with an incoming text as she was pulling on her knit sweater: I know what's going on. I have proof. Get over here.

There were also two missed calls from Feliz.

Juniper hit her voicemail and listened as she pulled on her coat and boots and then headed out the door. His voicemail was basically a reiteration of his text.

I know what's going on now. I have proof. Get over here so we can call the cops and get to the bottom of this.

***

"Feliz?" Juniper called as she closed the door behind her. The lights were all switched on, but he wasn't in the taproom. Probably still playing with his new recipe in the kitchen. Juniper crossed the plank floor to the other side of the taproom and pushed open the swinging door to the kitchen. The scent of cinnamon and vanilla made her mouth water. His latest custard creation sat on the stainless steel counter. A pot of milk had burned away on the stove. On the prep station there was lemon, cinnamon and egg yolks separated from the whites. It was odd he'd walk away with the stove still on and the eggs left out. Juniper switched the burner off and rinsed the pot, then went looking for Feliz.

He wasn't in the parlor, the dining room or upstairs. Juniper stopped outside the men's restroom and knocked on the door. Twice. It was empty. She stood in the hallway and tapped her foot. Then she went back down the hallway to the taproom. Where could he be? Surely, he wouldn't have taken off and left the place unlocked—especially after asking her to come down here. Could he have stepped outside for some fresh air? Not with milk on the stove. Juniper sat down at the piano and played around.

Ten minutes later, Feliz still hadn't returned.

She paced the foyer, and that's when something moved. Spooked, she jumped, plastering her back against the foyer's paneled wall.

When Juniper looked straight at the blur of movement, it disappeared. But in her peripheral vision she could see a woman in a long old-fashioned gown, motioning for Juniper to follow her into the basement. Juniper called out her chef's name again. Why had he bothered calling if he was going to leave? Juniper snatched her cell phone from her pocket and tapped his number on the speed dial with a lot more force than necessary.

The ghostly woman was more than a little unnerving, even for someone like Juniper.

Hopefully, he'd have a good explanation. Seconds later, the sound of a phone ringing made her jump. The sound was muffled, so she couldn't figure out where it was coming from. Instead, she followed the ghostly woman to the basement door. The sound got louder. The ringing seemed to come from downstairs in the basement. It made little sense that Feliz would be down there, especially in the dark. Juniper fumbled for the light switch and then tread carefully down the stairs, pausing at the midway point when the spirit disappeared. This was the same place Juniper had seen her earlier.

Gee, thanks for all the help. The ringing had stopped, and Feliz Merlot's voice mail picked up.

"Feliz?" Juniper hit the next light switch and the overhead bulbs blazed on. Juniper blinked a couple times at the sudden brightness. The door to the wine cellar was open.

Now what was going on here?

As Juniper moved inside the room, she spotted Feliz on the floor underneath one of the new wine racks that were meant to be installed upstairs behind the bar. He could be hurt. Her fight or flight kicked in and she raced to him. Her hands shook horribly as she lifted the wooden shelving. Then she recoiled in horror. There was a good reason why Feliz wasn't answering his phone.

AUTHORS NOTE:

Hello and welcome. Thank you for reading the first book in my new House Flipper series! I started writing this book on a whim several years ago. Just like Juniper, I'd come to a new town to live in a spooky old Victorian. That's right, Jack and Juniper's house is based on my own second empire although I have no secret tunnels—none that I'm willing to share, anyway. My new home is an hour away from the place I'd grown up in and while the change of pace was fun; it was harder than anticipated—being far from family, trapped in a creaky old house and alone with a busy toddler. On the surface, I was smiling, but on a deeper level I wondered if we'd made the right decision moving our children to a new place. Of course, we had, and we all settled in, eventually. In the meantime, in order to adjust I found myself writing about these house-flipping characters who were renovating just as we were and meeting quirky new characters just as I was. I'm happy to have found this house with all its history and this town with all its quirks and I'm so grateful that it inspired this mysterious tale.

As per usual, a big thanks to my family, friends, beta readers, reviewers and fans for their generosity and encouragement. Thanks to my awesome editor, Susan Croft. And of course, a big shout-out to my writing friends: our retreats are magical. Once again, thank you for reading my books. If you want more, please be sure to review them on Amazon so I can afford to continue. Come and say hello on my Facebook page, Twitter or my website.

With much gratitude,

Rachael

Bohemian Lake World *by series.* **The Bohemian Lake**
cozy mystery world comprised of multiple series. Each series focuses
on a different Bohemian resident (s), although all of the books
intersect.

A Penning Trouble Mystery
1. *Murder, She Floats*
2. *Murder, She Slopes*
3. *Murder, Ye Bones*
4. *Murder in the Catacombs*

Haunted House Flippers Inc.
1. *Cookies, Corpses & the Deadly Haunt*
2. *Candy Canes, Corpses & the Gothic Haunt*
3. *Crumb Cake, Corpses & the Run-of-the-Mill*
4. *Crème Eggs, Corpses & the Farmhouse Fixer*
5. *Black Cats, Corpses & the Pumpkin Pantry*
6. *Christmas, Corpses & the Gingerbread Flip Flop*

Bohemian Murder Manor Mysteries
1. *Gypsies, Traps & Missing Thieves*
2. *Make-Believes & Lost Memories*
3. *Ouija, Death & Wicked Witchery*
4. *Mistletoe & Hauntings*
5. *Ferris Wheels & Fortune Squeals*

Bohemian Festival Fiasco
1. *Bake or Die*
2. *Skate or Die* Coming 2021

Bookish Adventures in Witch-Lit
1. *Scandal & Gretel*
2. *Hyde & Seek*
3. *My Evil Valentine*
4. *Night of the Living Well-Read*

WORLD TIMELINE:

There are some people who have asked to read the books in the order in which they were written and published. If you are one of those people. You are welcome to read in this order if you don't mind jumping character story lines in order to stay in line with the seasons however reading by series will also work.

The mystery plots and character arcs are all independent of one another so any order can be read. I've linked the first book in every series for your convenience.

Optional Reading Order:

Book One: A Penning Trouble Mystery: Murder, She Floats
Book One: Haunted House Flippers: Cookies, Corpses & the Deadly Haunt
A Penning Trouble Mystery: *Murder, She Slopes*
Haunted House Flippers: *Candy Canes, Corpses & the Gothic Haunt*
Book One: Bohemian Murder Manor: Gypsies, Traps & Missing Thieves
Bohemian Murder Manor: *Make-Believes & Lost Memories*
Haunted House Flippers: *Crumb Cake, Corpses & the Run-of-the-Mill*
A Penning Trouble Mystery: *Murder, Ye Bones*
Book One: Bohemian Festival Fiasco: *Bake or Die*
Bohemian Murder Manor: *Ouija, Death & Wicked Witchery*
Haunted House Flippers: *Crème Eggs, Corpses & the Farmhouse Fixer*
Book One: Bookish Adventures in Witch-Lit: *Scandal & Gretel*
Bohemian Murder Manor: *Mistletoe and Hauntings*
Bookish Adventures in Witch-Lit: *Hyde & Seek*
A Penning Trouble Mystery: *Murder in the Catacombs*
Bookish Adventures in Witch-Lit: *My Evil Valentine*
Haunted House Flippers: *Black Cats, Corpses & the Pumpkin Pantry*
Bookish Adventures in Witch-Lit: *Night of the Living Well-Read*
Bohemian Murder Manor: *Ferris Wheels & Fortune Squeals*

Of course, as I said before, you may also continue to read in series order.

Next up for Haunted House Flippers is <u>Candy Canes, Corpses & the Gothic Haunt</u>

ABOUT THE AUTHOR

Rachael Stapleton lives in a Second-Empire Victorian with her husband, children and pets in Canada, eh! She delights in writing about all things cozy, whether it's a crisp autumn morning or hot chocolate by a crackling fire. Of course, she also loves the strange and unusual—murder, mayhem and wee ghosties. The fact that her house is the quintessential haunted old Victorian, resembling something out of a Scooby-doo episode could have something to do with it.

To get exclusive updates on new releases, giveaways, and exclusive content, subscribe to Rachael Stapleton's **Newsletter**.

Follow & Connect with Rachael:

Facebook | FB Group | Amazon |BookBub

Made in the USA
Thornton, CO
08/25/22 09:50:59

52e21623-4161-40a9-824e-f0d7bf72ce77R01